The Best Place
to Live Is
the Ceiling

A novel by

BARBARA WERSBA

The Best Place to Live Is the Ceiling

HARPER & ROW, PUBLISHERS, NEW YORK
Grand Rapids, Philadelphia, St. Louis, San Francisco
London, Singapore, Sydney, Tokyo, Toronto

Library of Congress Cataloging-in-Publication Data
Wersba, Barbara.
  The best place to live is the ceiling : a novel / by Barbara Wersba.
     p.   cm.
  "A Charlotte Zolotow book."
  Summary: A lonely teenager from Queens impulsively flies off to Switzerland on
another man's passport and finds his life turning into a James Bond adventure.
  ISBN 0-06-026408-X.—ISBN 0-06-026409-8 (lib. bdg.)
  [1. Mystery and detective stories. 2. Switzerland—Fiction.] I. Title.
PZ7.W473Bf   1990   90-30550
[Fic]—dc20   CIP
                                                                          AC

for Zue

The Best Place
to Live Is
the Ceiling

<u>February 10</u> Dr. Gutman, you have asked me to keep a notebook while I am seeing you, so I went out and bought this notebook. I think the idea is pointless, but will comply anyway. Where shall I begin? With Elizabeth Taylor, who I dreamed about last night? Why should I dream about Elizabeth Taylor? She's old enough to be my grandmother, and until recently was quite fat. Am I really so lonely that I should dream about having relationships with people who are in their fifties? The answer, of course, is yes. I am so lonely that I would have a relationship with Gloria Swanson, except that I think she's dead, and even if she weren't what would she want with a sixteen-year-old who may

3

be intelligent but who is still the only male virgin in his class.

"You have the highest IQ of anyone in the junior class," my guidance counselor said to me, in that reproving voice he has. But so what? Women do not go to bed with IQs. They go to bed with rippling muscles, and tan bodies, and prowess. I have all the prowess of a hibernating frog. If I said that to my father, he would reply that frogs turn into princes—but what can you expect of someone who teaches children's literature in a small college? To my father, the world is some sort of fairy tale, some sort of medieval adventure. To me, it is a prison.

I looked at myself in the mirror this morning and realized that what people always say about me is true. I look nineteen, or even older. I have a very mature look. But underneath this mature look is such a homely person that I cannot imagine any female ever wanting to know me. I have a big nose, bad skin, and thin blond hair. Woody Allen, who I resemble a little, at least has a sense of humor, a kind of dark wit. But for all the years I have been on this earth I have not been able to find a single virtue in myself, and this makes me think a lot about suicide.

When I contemplate my life, I feel terrible. My mother is dead, and my father and I live in Queens, New York, in an ugly little house with twelve stray cats. My father has a passion for cats and is always bringing home strays. We have had large cats, small cats, cats with no tails, crippled cats, pregnant cats, and cats who have lost their minds. The only activities my father and I do together are going to the vet or shopping for cat food at the supermarket. Either a cat is having a litter, or being spayed, or being wormed, and that is all we talk about. Except children's literature, of course. Other people's fathers are plumbers and carpenters, executives and dentists, but *my* dad spends his days involved in the inner meanings of *Mary Poppins*. He is completely obsessed with Mary Poppins and calls her "the cosmic nanny." He is also hooked on the works of Beatrix Potter ("the world seen small," he says) and has dozens of books on the life of Lewis Carroll. For years I have tried to pretend that I am not related to this man, that I don't know where he works or what he does, but to no avail. He thinks that *Alice in Wonderland* has existential meanings, and has said many times that *The Wind in the Willows* is an exploration of English social types.

Dr. Gutman, you said that I don't have to show this notebook to you. That I simply have to use it as a tool to explore my life. But the point is, I have very little life to explore. I've never been anywhere or done anything, have never smoked dope, or gotten drunk, or committed a crime. Which must make me unique in the history of adolescence. You did say last week that my constant need to sit in the restaurant at Kennedy Airport, and watch the planes take off, was unusual. But why is this unusual? Every time a 747 takes off for Paris or Rome, my heart goes into my throat—because somewhere in my mind's eye I can see myself, Archie Smith, getting on that plane. Shedding my life like a snakeskin, and starting over.

You once asked me if I had any obsessions, and of course I said no. But the truth is that I have been collecting travel brochures since I was twelve years old and have around three hundred of them. Brochures on Paris, Rome, London and Sydney. Booklets on New Zealand and Japan, Morocco and Greenland. I hang around travel agencies the way other people hang around discotheques, and can tell you the pros and cons of any airline in the world. I can also tell you the flying time to Lisbon and what

6

the best restaurants are in Cairo. Where to stay while you are in Frankfurt and how to rent a car in Hong Kong. Granted, that this is useless information—but just knowing it makes me feel better. With no trouble at all I can see myself boarding a 747 wearing terrific clothes and dark glasses, and carrying a briefcase. Because I am convinced, beyond the shadow of a doubt, that this single action would change my life. All I need, Dr. Gutman, is one small chance to start over and then I could succeed. Not that I would ever tell you this, because you'd think I'm crazy.

My father sent me to you three weeks ago because he does think I'm crazy. I'm supposed to have this very high IQ, and yet I barely got through the first two years of high school, and now I am having trouble getting through the third year of high school. I am rotten at sports, have few extracurricular activities, never go out with girls, and don't have any friends. My one and only friend, Clifford Tromblay, moved to Hawaii when we were both in the eighth grade, and that was the end of my interpersonal relationships.

How odd, Dr. Gutman, that I can say all these things to you in a notebook. In your office, I hardly

7

say anything. You and I sit staring at each other, and smiling at each other, and there doesn't seem much to say. I cannot tell you what is on my mind, because the thoughts are too bizarre and I don't want you to know them. I also don't want you to know how completely without hope I am, away from Kennedy Airport. Youth is supposed to be a time of hopefulness, but most of the time I feel like a very old man who bears a slight resemblance to Woody Allen.

Dr. Gutman, there is some graffiti on a cement wall near my school, and this graffiti says, "The best place to live is the ceiling." I agree, I agree, I agree.

February 14 I am a British double agent who resembles Richard Burton. The woman I am involved with is Audrey Hepburn. We are in postwar Berlin, and the person chasing us is Orson Welles. Psychotic. A killer. Atomic secrets are concealed beneath the skin of an apple in Audrey Hepburn's bag of groceries. In seeming innocence, we are returning from the grocery store in her quiet Berlin neighborhood. Suddenly an urchin runs up to us, upsets the bag of groceries, and steals the apple. From an empty window in a burned-out building, we can see Welles watching us, a high-powered rifle in his hands. He raises the rifle. . . .

This is the scenario I was creating today, Dr. Gutman, as you and I talked about the weather. The fact that we now talk about the weather makes me know that we have hit bottom. Any problems over the weekend? you asked. No, I said, everything's been fine. And then I sailed off into fantasy as you and I talked about the weather, and baseball, and the New York subway system. Your office is on Central Park West, in Manhattan, and it takes me an hour to get there, and then I have to travel an hour back home. Any problems? you asked. And I said no.

Well, let me tell you what the real problems are, Dr. Gutman. Let me just go through the events of yesterday. To begin with, my father woke up with the flu and phoned the college to cancel his classes. Which meant that I had to feed the cats. All of the cats. Lewie Carroll, who takes out his hostilities by peeing on the living room rug. Hans Christian, whom we first thought was a male, but who then had five babies. L. Frank Baum, who has epileptic fits. Newbery and Caldecott, who are still kittens and are destroying the furniture. J. M. Barrie, who throws up after every meal. The Brothers Grimm, who must be at least fourteen years old and have kidney trouble. Kipling, Tarkington, Thurber, and the Countess d'Aulnoy—who has a weight problem and is on diet medication.

Never let it be said that it is a simple thing to feed twelve cats when they all like different kinds of cat food. And never let it be said that it is a pleasant thing to change twelve litter boxes. After that, I had to give certain cats their medication, let others out into the yard, keep others in, supply the kittens with toys so they would lay off the furniture, and wash the dishes. By the time I was ready to leave for school, I was exhausted. I went into my father's room, to see if he needed anything before I left, and found him propped up in bed looking sorry for himself.

"I think I have a temperature," he said.

I took his temperature. He didn't.

"Could you fix me some soup and leave it on the stove? For lunch?"

I said I would do this.

"Maybe we could have Junket for dessert to-night," he said.

I looked at this man, whose name is Roger Dar-lington Smith, and who has been writing his Ph.D. dissertation for the last ten years, and felt not a twinge of pity. Because, Dr. Gutman, ever since my mother died, my father has been trying to turn me into a person who will cook and do dishes, vacuum and dust—and in all my fantasizing, the one thing I never fantasized being was a wife. It isn't that the man is mean—simply inept—and since it doesn't look like he will ever marry again, I have this image of me doing more and more housework, cooking more and more meals, until I turn into a transvestite. On the other hand, my father is a hard man to say no to because there is this pathetic streak in him—a quality which makes him trip over things on the sidewalk, miss trains, lose his glasses, wear his sweaters inside out, and get mugged every time he goes to Manhattan. He is in many ways a loser—but very intellectual, of course. Even today, with the flu, he had books and papers scattered all over the bed as he continued to work on the dissertation which I have begun to think of as a joke. How many years can a person write a doctoral thesis on the five volumes of *Mary Poppins*, Dr. Gutman? I ask you.

My father sneezed, blew his nose, and said, "I received a letter from Dr. Travers on Saturday."

Dr. Travers is P. L. Travers, who wrote *Mary Poppins*. My father has been corresponding with her for years.

"Good," I said lamely.

"What a woman. What a tremendous human being."

Then why don't you marry her? I wanted to say, and let her make you Junket and soup.

"The more we correspond, the more mysterious she becomes," my father said.

I was able to agree with this, Dr. Gutman. After all, it was P. L. Travers who once said in an interview, "I am a mere kitchenmaid in the house of myth and poetry." Figure that one out.

At any rate, I left my father in bed with his thesis, fixed some soup for him, missed the bus to school, took a taxi—which I cannot afford—was late to Spanish class, and was given hell by Señor Diego, the teacher. "What are you?" he kept asking me.

"Some kind of privileged character? Some kind of special human being?" All of which amused the members of Spanish II very much. Then I had a lousy lunch in the school cafeteria, was snubbed by a girl I am deeply attracted to, Betsy Graham, spilled a Coke down the front of my shirt, and realized that I was going to be late for Ancient History. I was hurrying down the corridor on the third floor, almost running, when Miss Morely, the principal's secretary, stopped me. "You!" she called. "You! Wait a minute."

Her voice was so urgent that I stopped. And would you believe this, Dr. Gutman? She thought I was the school janitor. Now I grant you that Miss Morely is very old and absentminded, but to mistake me for Clarence the janitor was wild. "The toilet is stopped up in the principal's office!" she said to me. "It's overflowing!" Rather than explain to her who I was, I said I would take care of it. But shall I tell you something, Dr. Gutman? I never got to Ancient History. The idea that anyone should take me for the school janitor was so depressing that I simply walked out of the building. I did not care what Mr. Wannings, the history teacher, would think. I did not care about anything. I only knew that I did not give a damn if the principal's toilet overflowed into Long Island Sound.

I passed the wall with the graffiti on it, the wall that says, "The best place to live is the ceiling," went into a park and sat down. It was a cold gray day, and I felt miserable. I thought about my father and P. L. Travers, who lives in London. I thought about the principal's toilet. Then, as a way of removing myself, I took out a dossier I am keeping on world travel and turned to a page I had titled *How to Behave in Foreign Countries*.

"In Latin American countries," I had written, "it is customary to be late for appointments, whereas the Swedes expect people to arrive on time. In Egypt, every service is rewarded with a tip, but do not tip in Japan. In Mexico, you should always inquire about a person's spouse. In Saudi Arabia, such questions are considered rude. In many Far Eastern countries, any object you admire will be given to you, so be careful what you admire."

I sat there reading this dossier, after which I tried to slip into one of my fantasies—tried to imagine myself a Russian spy, a famous polo player, a bullfighter, an Irish terrorist. I tried to see myself as a brilliant writer vacationing on the Riviera, or the world's youngest brain surgeon. I have been creating identities for years, Dr. Gutman, and sometimes I go around wearing disguises, except that nobody ever notices them. A particular hat, an old raincoat, a jaunty bow tie, a weird pair of shoes—these are enough to give me a persona. But today I couldn't come up with anything. I just sat there getting colder and colder, and then school was out and people were rushing past me. Normal, healthy, teenage people, none of whom needed to pretend he was a Russian spy. Betsy Graham came by with a person named Rick Olsen, who is very handsome and a jock, and they both looked at me as they passed, and smiled. It was a very pitying smile, Dr. Gutman, and so condescending—so completely condescending—that I knew I was coming towards the end of something. Quite possibly, my life.

February 16 Another session with you today. Another fifty dollars of my father's money down the drain. As usual, we talked about the weather and sports, and when you asked me how I was, I said fine. It's not that I dislike you, Dr. Gutman. For a psychologist, you're a pretty nice guy. Young. Good-looking. Sympathetic. But there's not a chance in the world that you will ever understand me, and so I do not reveal myself. One word to you about my fantasy life would probably result in incarceration. Mine, I mean. You would tell me I was psychotic or something. You would start writing in your little blue notebook.

We talked about sports and the weather while my mind kept returning to Betsy Graham and the smile she had given me the other day. It was a pitying smile, but there was a certain amount of pleasure in it. As though pitying *me* gave something extra to *her*. Why am I attracted to such a person? She isn't even beautiful. Well, actually she is. Thick auburn hair, freckles, pale pale skin. A gorgeous figure. Is she a virgin, Dr. Gutman? I doubt it. There is a steady look in her eyes that says she is not. I like the way she dresses. Like a wealthy hippie. And I like the way she moves—like a cat.

"You have mentioned several times that you like old movies." This is what you said today, Dr. Gutman, trying to draw me out. Like old movies? I *live*

16

for old movies—and if we didn't own a TV set, I would probably go out and steal one. There are no people on earth I identify with more than Cary Grant, Humphrey Bogart, Clark Gable, Robert Taylor, and all that group. And the women! Garbo, Bergman, Hepburn, Bette Davis, Joan Crawford. I have not had enough sleep since I was ten years old because of the Late Movie. I often pass out in class the next morning, making certain teachers think I'm a drug addict, but it's worth it. Last night, for the hundredth time, I watched *Casablanca*, and for the hundredth time found myself all choked up as Ingrid Bergman and Humphrey Bogart said goodbye at the airport. "Here's looking at *you*, kid." Has a better line ever been written?

"I don't feel much about old movies," I replied. "It's just something to do at night."

You sighed, Dr. Gutman, took off your glasses, and wiped them for a long time with your handkerchief. I could see that I was frustrating you, but I couldn't help it. I'm a very private person.

I left your office at four P.M.—and instead of going home, I took a bus out to Kennedy Airport. I had told my father that I was going to have dinner with

17

a friend from school, but of course it wasn't true. I just wanted to spend some time at the airport and watch the planes take off.

By now some of the waitresses at the Skyview Restaurant know me, but none of them seem to mind that I never order more than a sandwich and a Coke. This is a very attractive restaurant, with big windows facing the runways, and I sometimes think I could sit there forever. When a 747 comes in for a landing, it's like some kind of angry god dropping out of the sky. There's a shimmering haze all around the plane and it seems to be alive.

I sat there for a few hours, watching planes from all over the world take off and land, and observing people in the restaurant. Indian women in saris. Handsome black men who looked like diplomats. Delicate oriental people with their careful manners. Arabs, South Americans, people with English accents—a whole spectrum of people about to take off for exciting places where they would do exciting things. And suddenly I got so depressed that I just got up and left. Because I felt like a voyeur.

I didn't get home until nine o'clock, and of course my father was waiting up for me—a thing that drives me crazy. He still has the flu, and was sitting on the living room couch with four of the cats, and all of his books and papers. The TV was on, but he wasn't watching it. He was reading a book called *Pipers at the Gates of Dawn* and sneezing into a fistful of Kleenex. He was also wearing a bathrobe that must be twenty years old.

He gave me a watery smile. "I was worried about you, Archie."

"For God's sake," I said, sinking into a chair. "It's only nine o'clock."

"People get mugged in broad daylight."

"Well, I wasn't mugged."

"You must be careful on the city streets."

"I am, I am."

"How did the session go?"

"Fine," I said. "Terrific."

"You know, I've been reading the most wonderful book."

I didn't want to hear about a book—any book—but to be polite, I said, "Oh?"

"It's a series of interviews with children's book authors. Dr. Travers, of course, is represented."

"Of course. And what does she have to say?"

"It's complicated—because she is so involved with Eastern philosophy. But at one point in the

19

interview she says, 'I might as well be a clod in the forest with grass growing out of it, so at home do I feel in this world.' "

"Well," I said. "That's nice."

My father stared into space. "Some people think that Mary Poppins is simply a disguised version of Gurdjieff. It's an amazing idea."

I did not know who Gurdjieff was, Dr. Gutman, nor did I care. I went into the kitchen and brought out a bag of potato chips, sat down again, and began to munch. My father was writing some notes on a yellow legal pad, the TV was still going, and two of the cats—Lewie Carroll and Hans Christian— were about to have a fight.

Lewie Carroll and Hans Christian hated each other the minute they were introduced, a year ago, and they have had some violent confrontations. This evening they were sitting facing each other with their ears laid back, growling. Lewie extended one paw and braced it firmly against Hans Christian's forehead, and pushed. Hans Christian didn't give way. Lewie pushed harder, and Hans Christian winced but did not retreat. I didn't want to watch them fight, and I didn't want to separate them—so I went up to my room, thinking about my father and how overprotective he is. When he is not treating me like a housekeeper, he is treating me like a very small child, and in some ways I have less freedom than anyone I know. What I mean, Dr. Gutman, is that it is highly abnormal for someone sixteen years of age to have to phone home if he intends to be out after dark.

A good example of this is the time I went into the city to see a revival of *Mata Hari*, with Garbo, and sat through the movie three times. I knew that I was sitting through it three times, and yet on some other level I didn't—because I was spellbound. By nine that evening my father had gone berserk and had phoned the New York City police. "He went to an old Garbo film," he told the cops. "Somewhere on the West Side." But the police, being involved in more pressing matters, refused to search for me. And when I did get home that night, around eleven, my father was weeping.

Anyway. I entered my room, lay down on the bed, looked at the chaos around me, and picked up a travel supplement from the *Times* that I had been reading. "Picture yourself," said an ad for a cruise ship, "in a city of shimmering mosques and marble palaces. Or on a verdant hillside in Bali,

21

surrounded by ruined temples. Imagine yourself following the sun into the balmy waters of the equator, threading your way through 25 exotic ports of call. Close your eyes and see yourself in Dubrovnik, Malta, Odessa, Istanbul and Venice. Breathe in the perfumed excitement of the new, delight your palate with dishes that emperors have eaten."

I looked at my room again—at the shabby furniture, the travel posters on the wall, the piles of suspense novels, the mounds of sneakers, the cluttered bureau—and wondered how I could go on with my life for one more day.

February 17 Still depressed. Watched *Blood and Sand*, which I had never seen before. Famous old actress, Nazimova, played a small part.

February 18 Too depressed to write here. Watched *The Maltese Falcon*.

February 20 Can't write at all. Depressed.

February 21 Thinking of suicide, Dr. Gutman. So I cancelled my appointment with you.

February 24 Dr. Gutman, I am writing this entry from Zurich, Switzerland. No, I am not psychotic, and I am not lying. It is Friday, the 24th of February, and I am in Switzerland. I'm not kidding you. *I am*.

Here's what happened, and I hope I can describe it clearly because the whole thing is so fantastic that it's like one of those scenarios I invent while you talk about the weather. But this time it is real, Dr. Gutman. Real, actually happening. And to me.

Yesterday was Thursday, right? Having cancelled my appointment with you on Tuesday because of depression, I felt very lonely and adrift, so the following day I took this notebook and went over to the Skyview Restaurant to write down my thoughts and watch the planes take off. It was five in the afternoon and, as usual, I was sitting by the window having a sandwich and a Coke.

Suddenly the hostess came over to me, followed by a young man, and said, "Do you mind if this gentleman shares your table?" Well, I did mind—but since the restaurant was crowded, I said it would be OK. Just to be polite.

The man sat down—and the weird thing was, he resembled me. Exactly my height, with blond hair and a face that was a bit like mine, only of course he was handsome. He was around twenty years old, and so expensively dressed that I couldn't help staring at him. Tight jeans—designer jeans, probably—suede boots, a gray cashmere turtleneck sweater, and a gray suede Windbreaker. Then I saw that he was wearing a purse, Dr. Gutman, a *purse*, and decided that he must be gay. It was a flat black purse that went over his shoulder on a strap.

He smiled, picked up the menu and said, "Thanks, old buddy. I appreciate it." He was talking about the shared table, but the minute he spoke I knew he wasn't gay. He was very macho, very cool.

I observed him closely, and then I stared at his purse again. The initials "B.C." were stamped on it in gold, so of course the first thing that came to my mind was "Before Christ." Totally wrong, of course.

B.C. had ordered scotch on the rocks and a club sandwich. "Going abroad?" he asked me. "Uh, no," I said. "Not tonight."

There was a pause, so to keep things going, I said, "Are *you* going abroad?"

He took a handful of peanuts and nodded. "Switzerland. A skiing vacation."

"Well," I said. "That's nice."

"You ski?"

"Uh, not recently. Not for a while."

"I try to ski the Parsenn twice a year. Have to spend a few days in Zurich first, however."

I didn't know what the Parsenn was, Dr. Gutman, but the idea that this guy went to Europe twice a year absolutely amazed me. I decided that he must be an actor, or some kind of celebrity. He had a very theatrical voice.

"What's your opinion of Zurich?" I asked, trying to sound casual.

"If one *has* to go abroad, it's a pretty good place," he replied. "Small, cosmopolitan, urbane."

25

"Right," I said. "Urbane."

B.C.'s scotch arrived. He took a sip of it and gave me a tolerant smile. "What I always say is . . ."

He didn't finish the sentence. As a matter of fact, he didn't finish anything. Because all of a sudden he went very pale—I mean, pale like death—and clutched at his chest. "God," he said, "I think I'm . . ."

And then he fell to the floor.

Dr. Gutman, I am not a person who reacts well in an emergency. So I just sat there staring at this guy, who by now was lying unconscious on the floor, as everyone else snapped into action. The waitresses. Other patrons. The manager of the restaurant. They tried to revive B.C. with cold cloths on his forehead and mouth-to-mouth resuscitation. When none of this worked, they called an ambulance.

In about five minutes two paramedics appeared and lifted B.C. onto a stretcher. I watched them carry him out, and then I looked down and saw that his purse had fallen to the floor. I picked it up, and was just about to run after the paramedics when the loudspeaker said, "Swissair flight 100 now boarding

26

at gate 32. We repeat. Flight 100 for Zurich now boarding."

I stood there for a minute without fully understanding my situation. When I did understand it, my heart began to pound.

I opened B.C.'s purse and found the following. A passport with the name Brian Chesterfield on it. Two thousand dollars' worth of traveler's checks. Three thousand dollars in American money. A letter of reservation from a place called the Hotel Opera— and a plane ticket to Zurich with a luggage check attached. In the purse were also a boarding pass, a small red address book, and a photo of a woman. Irrelevantly, it crossed my mind that B.C. had had to carry a purse because his jeans were so tight.

"Will all passengers for Swissair flight 100, New York to Zurich, please report to gate 32," the loudspeaker said.

My ticket said "flight 100," so I made my way out of the restaurant with Brian Chesterfield's black purse over my shoulder. I knew exactly where gate 32 was, because I knew this airport like the back of my hand. I also knew that my heart was pounding like a sledgehammer.

It was a long walk to gate 32, and as I proceeded down the corridor my life passed before my eyes. I saw myself in kindergarten, standing in a corner, afraid to talk to anyone. I saw myself in the first grade, the only person in the whole school named Archibald. I saw myself in the seventh grade at recess time, the last one chosen for every team. I saw myself lurching into adolescence, sex-ridden and miserable. "Rest in peace," I said to Brian Chesterfield. Because I was sure he was dead, Dr. Gutman. Almost positive.

I reached gate 32 and entered the passenger lounge, where hundreds of people were milling about. Rich-looking people, poor-looking people, people with babies, people on canes, fat people, thin people, terribly old people—and all of them waiting to board a plane to Zurich. I sat down in a comfortable chair and put Brian Chesterfield's purse on my lap. The lady sitting opposite me smiled.

Suddenly everyone was lining up near a big door, so I got in line too, wondering how so many people could fit on one plane. Then we were proceeding down a corridor, and finally—one by one—we went through an electronic device which would show whether or not we were carrying bombs. I go into all this detail because, believe it or not, I had never been on a plane before.

Another corridor, carpeted in blue—and then we were going under a kind of canopy into the aircraft. I saw that people were showing their boarding passes at the entrance, so I showed mine too. A stewardess pointed out my seat, which was in the middle of the plane, on the left side, by a window.

This plane was not like a plane. It was like a hotel. Hundreds of seats, sections for smoking or non-smoking, whole banks of kitchens and bathrooms. I was amazed by it, and crawled into my seat over the lap of a man who was reading *Time* magazine. "Zurich," I said to myself. "Switzerland."

Life is ironic, Dr. Gutman, because of all the countries in the world, the one country I knew nothing about was Switzerland. I mean—nothing. So I tried to calm myself and come up with something. Cows, chocolates, wristwatches. And that was all I could remember. I wasn't even sure where Switzerland was. Somewhere in the middle of Europe, covered with Alps.

Even though people were in their seats by now, I knew that there was still time for me to get off the plane. I did not have to go to a country filled with cows and wristwatches. I could change my mind and debark.

Then I remembered a thriller I had read once, in which a character says, "On the streets of Zurich, every third man is a spy."

I didn't know what to do. Half of me wanted to get off the plane, and half of me wanted to stay. At any rate, the choice was made for me, because all of a sudden stewardesses were closing doors and the engines were revving up. I began to sweat and feel faint—that's how severe my panic was. Yet at the same time, I knew that something wonderful was happening.

I was sitting by the window, the man who was reading *Time* was sitting on the aisle, and the middle seat was empty. I was about to put my purse on it when I saw a woman in a fur coat rushing up the aisle. Sure enough, she climbed over the man who was reading *Time* and plumped down in the empty seat. "Too late, almost!" she said to me. "Incredible."

She wriggled out of her fur coat and gave me such a dazzling smile that I liked her at once. She must have been around forty and was wearing a beige wool suit. Her hair was perfectly done, and there was a big diamond ring on her finger. I wondered if she was a celebrity.

"A jam of traffic," she said. "The cab sitting there for *hours*."

I nodded as though I knew what she meant—and, because she was fastening her seat belt, I fastened mine. Then the plane took off, and I have never in my life had such a sensation. This giant hotel with around four hundred people in it simply roared straight up into the sky. In two minutes we were over New York.

The "no smoking" sign flashed off, so the woman in the fur coat lit a long black cigaret and gave me another smile. "You go to Zurich or Geneva? We stop in Geneva first."

"Zurich," I said. "A skiing vacation."

"How lovely. How very very nice. My husband was once a skier of excellence. Now, of course, too old."

"Of course," I said, wondering what kind of accent she had. It was slightly German and slightly English. I couldn't tell which.

"Permit me an introduction. I am Melina Mendelsohn."

"How do you do?" I said. "My name is Brian Chesterfield." We shook hands.

At that point, one of the stewardesses gave us a demonstration of how to use the emergency oxygen masks and life jackets—and then more stewardesses came around with magazines and newspapers. After that, *more* stewardesses moved up and down the aisles taking orders for drinks. "You must allow me to buy you some champagne," Mrs. Mendelsohn said. "It would be festive."

"Well," I said. "Thank you."

"You have been abroad many times?" she asked, after she had placed the order.

Suddenly I decided to take a chance on this woman. "No," I said. "This is the first time."

She clasped her hands to her bosom. "The first time! How wonderful. You will ski, you will meet the girls, you will enjoy yourself. But the Swiss, I must warn you, are odd. Very guilt-ridden, very self-conscious. They do not believe in pleasure, so it makes them neurotic. Their scenery, however, is splendid."

Our champagne arrived, and Mrs. Mendelsohn raised her glass to me. "To your first trip abroad! To health and happiness."

Dr. Gutman, that moment was the closest I had come to crying in a long long time. The fact that this beautiful woman was toasting me with a glass of champagne, on a flight to Europe, was just so fantastic that I almost sobbed. I loved Mrs. Mendelsohn. I could have married her.

We had two glasses of champagne and talked right through dinner, which was chicken and potatoes, vegetables, salad, rolls, and a terrific chocolate-pudding dessert. Mrs. Mendelsohn's husband was a businessman. They lived in Zurich and had a weekend house in a town called Klosters. Her married children lived in New York—so she came and went. That is the expression she used, Dr. Gutman, "came and went." As though to commute between Zurich and New York was nothing. She also told me that she had been an opera singer in her youth and had traveled around the world three times.

After dinner, a wall panel in our section of the plane went up—and a movie began. And the fact that it was a James Bond movie was significant to me because I am a Bond addict. Mrs. Mendelsohn watched the film with as much interest as I did, and then a stewardess brought us pillows and blankets.

The lights in the plane lowered, everything was suddenly quiet above the steady sound of the engines, and Mrs. Mendelsohn and I went to sleep.

I woke at dawn to see a field of white clouds and a thin band of gold on the horizon. And when the pilot, in his strange accent, announced that we were over Ireland, a lump came into my throat. I, Archie Smith, had just crossed the Atlantic.

A stewardess brought us hot cloths to wipe our faces with, and then some orange juice—and Mrs. Mendelsohn went off to the bathroom to fix her hair and makeup. "On your left," said the pilot's voice over the loudspeaker, "you will see the city of Paris and the river Seine."

Forty-five minutes later we were coming in for a landing at Geneva. But though I stared and stared out the window, all I could see was fog. A dull-looking airport, and fog. The plane took off again and within a half hour we were landing at Kloten Airport in Zurich, also in the fog, and people were crowding the aisles trying to get their coats on. I helped Mrs. Mendelsohn into her fur coat, aware— for the first time—of how crummy I must look. All I was wearing were blue jeans, jogging shoes, an old sweater and a duffel coat.

"Where will you ski?" Mrs. Mendelsohn asked me. "Davos? St. Moritz?"

"Both," I said quickly.

"Then you go directly to the Alps?"

"Uh, no. Zurich first. The Hotel Opera."

"Dufourstrasse," she said. "A very sensible street. You will walk around the lake and feed the swans. You will eat in the good local restaurants."

As we moved down the aisle of the plane, my mind began to race. I would have to pick up B.C.'s luggage. I would have to find my way into Zurich and change my American dollars into Swiss money, whatever that was. I would have to convince the Hotel Opera that I was a wealthy young American on vacation. These were all the things I considered, Dr. Gutman. The one thing I did *not* consider was that we were about to go through Passport Control.

The official in the glass booth studied Mrs. Mendelsohn's passport, nodded, and gave it back to her. Then it was my turn, and as I slid my passport across the counter to him, I began to sweat. But—amazingly—this man didn't even glance at B.C.'s photo on the front page. He merely looked at the date on the passport, nodded, and I was home free.

Mrs. Mendelsohn and I walked through the huge

airport, went down two escalators, and finally wound up at the luggage reception—where everyone's bags were going around on a revolving belt. Once again I panicked, as I realized that I didn't know what B.C.'s bags looked like. People were grabbing their luggage off the belt—Mrs. Mendelsohn found hers at once—and the only thing I could think of was to delay, to wait until there were only a few bags left and then compare luggage checks.

"I don't see my bags yet," I said. "Maybe you should go on without me."

"I would not hear of it!" Mrs. Mendelsohn replied. "We will have a cigaret together and wait for the missing bags. Then I will guide you into Zurich."

She gave me one of her beautiful smiles, Dr. Gutman, and for one moment I thought she was on to me. Then I decided that she was simply a very kind, very generous woman. It was terrible that we weren't the same age.

To make a long story short, we had a cigaret together (though I rarely smoke) and walked around the airport for a while. When we returned to the luggage belt, B.C.'s lone suitcase was going round and round, so we retrieved it, went downstairs to a platform that was like an elegant version of a New

York subway station—and took the train into Zurich. "You are on foreign soil," I said silently to myself. "You are in Europe."

Mrs. Mendelsohn was chatting away with such animation—telling me about her daughter who had just married the first violinist of the New York Philharmonic—that I had trouble concentrating on the scenery. But when there was a lull in the conversation, I looked out of the train window and received a shock. The neighborhoods we were passing were filled with dreary-looking shops and small factories. The whole thing resembled Queens.

The train pulled into a railway station. The biggest, coldest, most impressive railway station I had ever seen, with hundreds of people hurrying back and forth, and food counters and newsstands, and restaurants and shops, and whole flocks of sparrows flying up near the glass-domed ceiling. I stared at all this as Mrs. Mendelsohn led me over to a booth to change my American dollars into Swiss money. Once again the man in the booth looked at my passport without really seeing it, and I cashed one thousand dollars into large, beautiful Swiss francs. They did not look like money, they looked like paintings. B.C.'s traveler's checks, however, I did

37

not touch. Some instinct told me that it would be dangerous to cash them.

I allowed Mrs. Mendelsohn to guide me out of the station and push me gently into a cab. "The treat is on me," she said. "I will drop you at your hotel, and then continue to my house on the Zurichberg. The driver will go slowly. You will see the sights."

The cab wound through the busy streets, went to the right, went to the left, and then—suddenly—I saw a city that was built on the banks of a narrow river, saw ancient buildings and spires, and heard church bells ringing. Mrs. Mendelsohn was conducting a kind of tour for me ("This side of the river is called the Limmatquai, and soon we will pass the historic Water Chapel. On the other side, you can see the spires of Fraumunster and St. Peter's.") but I barely heard her. All I could do was gaze at the swans that were sailing down the river, and listen to the bells, and stare at the beautiful buildings. "Those are the old guild halls," Mrs. Mendelsohn was saying. "And there, on your left, is Grossmunster, the famous cathedral. This river you are admiring opens out to the Zurichsee, Lake Zurich, and beyond, of course, are the Alps."

In about five minutes the cab had pulled up in front of the Hotel Opera, and Mrs. Mendelsohn was helping me out with my bag. As we stood on the pavement together, she took a pad and pencil from her purse. "I am writing down for you my two phone numbers. One in Zurich, the other in Klosters. You will call me and we will reestablish ourselves. For the next ten days, however, I am in Lugano."

"Where?"

"Lugano, in the Ticino, near Italy. My cousin, alas, is very ill and I must visit him."

"You mean that you'll be away for ten days?"

Mrs. Mendelsohn laughed. "My dear, enjoy your holiday. When you return from skiing, I will buy you a cup of tea at Sprungli's."

She kissed me on both cheeks, gave a little wave, and swept back into the cab. And then I was standing alone on the steps of the Hotel Opera.

Dr. Gutman, this was a very small hotel, not at all like the ones in New York, but I could not bring myself to go inside. Anxiety was washing over me in waves, and for the first time I wondered what I had done. I was using another man's passport and had just changed one thousand dollars of his money into Swiss francs. I had deserted my father, who had probably called the police by now. I had left school in the middle of my junior year, and would undoubtedly be expelled when I returned—if I returned. I was already a kind of criminal. And for what? I asked myself. *For what?*

February 25 Dr. Gutman, it is Saturday morning, ten A.M. Zurich time, and I have just finished a beautiful breakfast served to me in my hotel room by a beautiful maid. My room is on the second floor, with a view of the lake, and because we are just behind the opera house, sets from operas keep passing on open trucks beneath my window. A whole forest went by yesterday, followed by a small castle. My room is so elegant that it almost defies description, but I will try. Two beautiful beds with down comforters on them instead of blankets. A tiny snack bar, with refrigerator, filled with snacks and cold drinks. A futuristic red-and-white-tiled bathroom, with a narrow deep tub and free packets of bubble bath. I have a color television set, and have watched a number of American movies dubbed into other languages. Very amusing, to say the least, to watch

Katharine Hepburn and Spencer Tracy speaking German. Or to hear Bette Davis ranting and raving in Italian.

There is an alcove in my room that has a breakfast table in it, and so I have my breakfast of café au lait and fresh rolls looking out the tall windows at Lake Zurich, one block away. At eleven each morning a maid knocks on my door and asks, in Italian, if she can do my room. The languages here confused me until I learned that four are spoken in this country. Swiss German, Italian, French, and something called Romansch. This is my life now, Dr. Gutman, a life of complete luxury—and since I will probably be going to jail when I return to America, I have decided to enjoy things while I can. I will continue to keep this journal so that you can read it while I'm doing time.

Zurich is so fantastic. So beautiful.

Here is what happened on Thursday, when I finally entered the hotel. The receptionist—whose name is Marie and who speaks English—asked for my passport, but once again didn't study it. I signed a registration form as Brian Chesterfield, from New York City, and a bellboy took my suitcase up to my room. No one in the hotel looked at me as though

I were a teenager adrift in Zurich. As a matter of fact, no one looked at me at all.

The minute I was alone in the hotel room, I opened B.C.'s suitcase, which wasn't locked. And this is what I found. One pair of pajamas and one wool bathrobe. One black sweater. A change of underwear and a shaving kit. A comb, brush, toothbrush, and one small tube of Colgate. Then it hit me—no ski clothes. And no skis. B.C. had said that he was going skiing, but had no equipment.

It was eleven in the morning Zurich time, and five A.M. New York time—which was probably why I felt exhausted. So I took off my clothes, had a bubble bath, dried myself with a thick white towel, and went to bed. And the minute I rolled up in one of the down comforters, I was asleep. When I woke, it was three P.M., Zurich time, and all I could think of was my father.

I dressed and went downstairs to the desk, wondering how I could make a phone call to New York. "Should I phone from my room?" I asked Marie. "*Nein, nein,*" she said. "Much too expensive. It will be better for you to phone from the post office, or the central railway station."

She told me how to find the Hauptbahnhof, the

station that Mrs. Mendelsohn and I had been in a few hours earlier, and so I set out on foot. I suppose I could have taken a streetcar—there were little blue streetcars crisscrossing the entire city—but I felt better on foot. It was freezing cold, and I knew that I would have to buy warmer clothes. Then I saw that lots of the men on the street were wearing purses, so I sent up a prayer of apology to B.C. It was, of course, beginning to occur to me that he might not be dead at all.

It was raining now, a cold thin rain, but I didn't care because I was crossing a bridge called the Quaibrucke, with Lake Zurich on one side and the River Limmat on the other, and flocks of sea gulls were wheeling over my head, and church bells were ringing, and everything looked wonderful in the gloom. The older people I passed looked very much like the ones back home, but the kids were weird. Absolutely and totally weird.

Soon I was walking down the Bahnhofstrasse, Dr. Gutman, which is the most gorgeous street I have ever seen. Jewelry stores, department stores, boutiques, bookstores, dozens of banks—and no cars allowed, just the narrow blue trams. No one seemed to be in a hurry, like they are in New York, and

almost everyone had a dog. At the end of this long
street was an escalator which took me down into a
shopping mall, just as Marie had described, and
then I took another escalator up—into the railway
station.

It was very simple to phone home. I entered a
huge room filled with phone booths, went up to the
desk, and was told by a man who spoke English
which booth to use, and how to dial. Three minutes
would cost ten francs.

I dialed my own number and felt the sweat beginning to run down my neck. My father answered
almost at once. "Hello, hello?" he said. He sounded
desperate.

"Daddy?" I said. "It's me. I'm all right."

"*Archie?* Is it you? I can't hear you."

"It's me, Dad. And I'm OK. Really. I'm sorry you
were worried."

There was a sob on the other end of the phone.
"Worried? You've been missing for hours. I called
the police."

"I'm sorry, Dad."

"Where are you, Archie? You sound so far away."

I took a deep breath and said, "Well, in one sense
I *am* far away. I'm in Switzerland."

There was a long pause. "Where?" he said.

"Switzerland. I'm calling from the Hauptbahnhof in Zurich. It's raining here."

"I'm in no mood for jokes, Archie."

"I'm not joking. I took a plane here yesterday. Swissair. It was a lovely flight."

"Archie, I'm not a well man. I have the flu and a temperature of one hundred, and . . ."

"Dad, listen. This is kind of expensive, so I'll put the whole thing in a letter to you. OK? How are the cats?"

"The cats are fine," he said in a cold voice.

"Good. I'm glad to hear it. Take care of your flu now, you hear me? So long, Dad."

I strolled back down the Bahnhofstrasse, part of me feeling guilty and the other part feeling wonderful. No more arguments about coming in late at night, no more visits to psychologists or sessions with guidance counselors. No more cats, dishes, boxes of kitty litter, or trips to the supermarket. For the first time in sixteen years, I was free.

February 26 Momentary panic. Went down to the

lobby this morning to find a note in my mailbox. "Kindly call Herr Gessner. 47–35–39." What to do? Nothing. Ignore it. Also startled when Marie, at the desk, asked if I wished to stay at the hotel longer than three days—the length of B.C.'s reservation. I said yes, I would stay longer.

February 27 Bought new clothes—a James Bond-looking raincoat, corduroy pants, a turtleneck sweater, and a visored cap. Man in the store didn't speak English, but was helpful anyway. (I am beginning to understand the Swiss money!) Went to a restaurant on the Limmatquai in these clothes, feeling terrific. Ordered a glass of beer (no one asked for an I.D.) and sat there for a long time, listening to the different languages around me and observing people. If Mrs. Mendelsohn had only been with me, everything would have been perfect. I miss her with a pain that is almost physical, Dr. Gutman. Which is crazy, because we only knew each other for a few hours.

Another thing I did today was to buy the following things at a bookstore. A map of Switzerland. A guidebook about Zurich. And the *International Traveler's Pocket Dictionary and Phrase Book, German/English*. All very helpful, particularly the phrase book. I have already memorized one sentence—*Ist dieser Käse sehr scharf?*—which means Is this cheese very strong?—and intend to memorize at least ten sentences a day. Marie, at the desk, has explained to me that while the spoken language of Zurich is Swiss German (Schweizerdeutsch) and while the written language is regular German, people understand both. Very complicated, but I intend to master the whole thing because I am crazy about it here.

Suppose I never went home, Dr. Gutman. Suppose I just stayed, and learned the language and got a job. Would the world fall apart? Would Queens, New York, grind to a halt? No. After a while no one, except my father, would even miss me. The point is, I am in love with this city—the medieval buildings, the clanging church bells, the gloomy gray skies, and the food shops with their incredible displays. There are breeding pens for swans along the river, and people come to the stone steps with bags of bread and corn for them. At night the water is velvet black, with gold lights shining in it. The great churches—Fraumunster, Grossmunster, St. Peter's—are lit up, and when I walk home from dinner the swans are still gliding by in the darkness.

Observations Despite the fact that Zurich is covered with graffiti, everyone here seems obsessed with cleanliness. In every neighborhood there are men in orange work clothes sweeping the sidewalks, and, unlike New York, people do not litter. Everyone is polite. People shake hands upon arriving or departing. Even tiny children.

All of the cars are beautiful—Lancias, Citroëns, Mercedes—but there seems to be no speed limit. People drive like maniacs until they come to a traffic light, then they screech to a halt. The streetcars have an honor system. You buy your ticket at a machine on the sidewalk, but no one on the car comes around to collect it. Amazing.

No matter what you say to people here, they reply, "Ja, ja."

The music on the radio in my hotel room is mostly very weird rock and roll. In the late afternoon, there are entire programs devoted to yodeling.

People are more flirtatious here than at home. They kiss and hold hands on the street. Even the middle-aged.

Everyone seems to hang clothes out overnight on the apartment balconies. Don't know why.

In restaurants, people always ask, Is this seat free? before sitting down at your table. Also, a person can sit over a cup of coffee for hours without being disturbed.

The Swiss seem to like babies and dogs more than they like each other.

February 29 (Leap year) Another note in my mail-box. "Urgent that you call Herr Gessner. 47–35–39." Don't know what to do about this, as Herr

Gessner is undoubtedly a personal friend of B.C. Very disturbing. B.C. is on my mind constantly these days. I have images of him in a hospital somewhere, paralyzed, worrying about his black purse and his traveler's checks.

Decided not to write my father a letter, because there is no way of explaining my situation to him. Have sent him a series of enigmatic postcards instead. Have also sent enigmatic postcards to Betsy Graham, Rick Olsen, my guidance counselor Mr. Murphy, and to you, Dr. Gutman.

Mrs. Mendelsohn will be back in four days.

I have been here less than a week, but have already done the following things. Bought a black leather jacket on Theater Street. Had lunch at Sprungli's, the shop Mrs. Mendelsohn mentioned to me, where they have fantastic pastries. Asked for the menu in German—*Die Speisekarte, bitte*—and was understood! I have walked around the lake, to the opposite side, where there is a huge stone lion sitting on a pedestal in the water. I have been to a pornographic movie called *Anguish and Black Lace* (my translation) which shocked the hell out of me. And I have had a glass of wine at the Cafe Odeon, near Bellevue, which is an artists' hangout. High ceilings, mirrors, marble tables, potted palms—and the most bizarre kids I have ever seen.

Dr. Gutman, the kids in Zurich are not like the ones in New York. As a matter of fact, the kids in Zurich are not like the ones anywhere. All of them wear one uniform—boots, jeans, layers of sweaters, beat-up jackets and a cotton scarf wound around the neck—and all of them have punk hairdos. Crew cuts dyed purple or yellow, or normal hair with a violent streak of color down the front. Most of the boys wear one earring, and everyone—I mean, everyone—is stoned.

These kids give concerts in the streets, hand out political literature, hang around the pinball machine parlors along the Limmatquai, or beg for money on the Bahnhofstrasse. In the six days that I've been here I have seen them sleeping on the ground near the Quaibrucke, or sitting huddled together in St. Peter's Square smoking dope. It is beginning to occur to me that *they* are the ones who have covered Zurich with graffiti, but I don't know why.

March 2 Something has happened. At six this morning my phone rang—and it was Herr Gessner, who has been leaving all those messages for me. As you might imagine, I was sound asleep and at first didn't know what was happening.

"Herr Chesterfield?" the voice said. "This is Gessner speaking."

"What?" I said, fumbling for the light on the bedside table. "Hello?"

"I am addressing Herr Brian Chesterfield?"

"Yes," I said.

"Then permit me to welcome you to Zurich, Herr Chesterfield. Your very good friends have been waiting for you. The fact that you have not phoned them is a bewilderment."

"My friends?"

A note of annoyance crept into the voice. "I am addressing Herr Brian Chesterfield? From New York?"

"Uh, no," I said. "Actually, you're not. This is his roommate."

By now, Dr. Gutman, I was wide awake. Because this man's voice was ominous—very gruff, with a thick German accent. Also, it was six in the morning. Not a time when you normally phone people.

"My name is Rick Olsen," I said. "I am Mr. Chesterfield's companion. Mr. Chesterfield is in Lugano at the moment."

There was a pause on the other end of the phone. "I am sorry to hear that, Herr Olsen. Very sorry indeed. What message shall I give to Herr Chesterfield's very good friends?"

"Well . . ." I said. "Just say hello to them. Or bon voyage. Something like that." And then I hung up.

I was so rattled by this phone call that I got out of bed, dressed, and sat by the window—watching the dawn come up over Lake Zurich. There was something about Herr Gessner's voice that scared the hell out of me, and suddenly I decided to have breakfast in a restaurant instead of my room.

I had eggs and bacon in a local coffeehouse, walked down to the Limmatquai, crossed a bridge, and made my way up to a square called the Lindenhof—which I had read about in my guidebook. "The Lindenhof!" said the guidebook. "It soars twice the height of the old roofs of the town, crowning the fortifications of the past. It is surrounded by narrow lanes which lead to a promenade bathed in the shadow of linden trees. There, on the benches, many a famous person has sat in reverie."

When I had climbed to the Lindenhof I sat down on a bench and tried to compose myself. I couldn't figure out whether B.C. was in trouble, or whether he simply had some very strange friends. Either way, the whole thing made me nervous.

Before me, the city of Zurich was spread out like a panorama—tiled roofs, chimneys, church steeples, the towers of the Grossmunster just across the river, and the university buildings beyond. Sunlight was breaking through the steel-gray clouds, and the whole sight was very beautiful. Across the square from me, near a synagogue, was an old lady on a cane—also staring at the view. She turned, headed towards me, and as she passed the bench where I was sitting she gave a little bow and said something that sounded like, "Grootzie."

All of a sudden I realized that this was the first person in Zurich who had spoken to me. Outside of Marie, at the desk. So I jumped to my feet and bowed back, and said, *"Guten Morgen."* She smiled and bowed again, and *I* bowed again—and as she hobbled away this terrible sadness came over me. Loneliness, I guess.

I followed a narrow street back down to the river, where I fed my breakfast roll to a couple of swans.

After that, I went to a place called the Schweizer Heimatwerk, which is a crafts shop, and bought a Swiss Army Knife and a small cowbell. The depression I felt was getting worse, so I decided to go over to the central railway station and have lunch. This station, the Hauptbahnhof, is like a small city—with restaurants and shops, and even a movie theater. It was the place where I had phoned my father, and where I now mailed postcards and changed money.

I bought an English magazine at a newsstand, and was just heading towards a restaurant when a girl approached me. The shabbiest, dirtiest girl I had seen thus far in Zurich. She looked around twelve years old, was dressed in filthy jeans and an old army jacket, and had a crew cut dyed orange.

She said something in German that I could not understand—but it was clear she wanted money. And for some reason, that made me mad. Why, I thought, should I give her B.C.'s hard-earned money? Why the hell doesn't she get a job and earn some? All of which—I admit—was irrational of me.

I didn't want this girl to know I was an American, so I shook my head very calmly and said, "*Es tut mir leid,*" which means I'm sorry.

She looked surprised. *"Was?"*

"Es tut mir leid."

She said something that sounded like *"Ich habe Hunger,"* and once again I shook my head.

"Ich habe Hunger!" she said more loudly.

I began to move away from her. "I'm sorry," I said. "Really."

"Sorrie?" she yelled in a thick German accent. *"Sorrie?* Fuck you, mister."

I was so depressed by this encounter that I decided to go back to the hotel. And there, in my mailbox, was a postcard from Mrs. Mendelsohn. When I saw the signature on the card, my heart leapt. But then I read the message.

My dear, If you are still at the Hotel Opera, I send you warm greetings. My cousin is in grave health, so I must remain in Lugano for a time. *Auf Wiedersehen*. Melina Mendelsohn.

March 5 Dr. Gutman, there is a girl sleeping in my room. Yes, that is what I said—a girl. The one who tried to beg from me in the railway station. She is here at this very moment, asleep in one of my twin beds, and I have no idea how to get rid of her. But that is not what I want to talk about. The important thing is what happened two days ago with Herr Ulrich Gessner.

I was so upset by Mrs. Mendelsohn's postcard that I stayed in bed late that day, thinking about her and wondering how I could be attracted to someone her age. "You go out of your way to make life hard for yourself," my guidance counselor had once said to me—and I was beginning to think he was right.

Around eleven o'clock the girl who cleans the rooms wanted to clean mine, so I showered and dressed, ate my breakfast rolls, and went down to the lobby. Marie, at the desk, said, "Good morning, Herr Chesterfield," and I said good morning back to her.

Then I saw the man.

He was sitting in the lobby reading a newspaper, but when Marie said good morning to me, he looked up quickly. He was wearing a brown leather coat and a brown beret, and was rather fat. The point is, Dr. Gutman, when I left the hotel, he left too.

57

I began to walk very quickly towards Bellevue. And when I looked back, the man was following me. I began to run—and so did he.

Soon we were both running along the Limmatquai, and I was starting to panic. I knew he thought I was Brian Chesterfield, and I also knew that he was out to get me—maybe even to murder me. I *also* knew that his name was Gessner.

He began to gain ground on me near the Grossmunster, so I darted into one of the side streets and headed up a small hill. I didn't know where I was, but all of a sudden the whole atmosphere was different—discos, porno shops, pizza parlors, and street people everywhere. Kids were sitting on benches, smoking dope or playing guitars, and there were a lot of dogs running around.

I flung myself into the first doorway I saw, which turned out to be a place called The Red Light House. "Fun, sex, and cool drinks," the sign said—but I was not about to be fussy. All I knew was that I had to lose the man in the leather coat.

The place was so dark that at first I couldn't see anything. But when my eyes adjusted to the dim light, I saw that I was in a bar. There was a jukebox playing terrible rock and roll, and all these weird types were standing at the bar drinking.

When I say weird, Dr. Gutman, I do mean weird—because I had never seen any people like these before. Girls wearing leather miniskirts and too much makeup. Men wearing necklaces and eye shadow. There was a woman dressed like a man, in a pinstriped suit, and another woman sitting at the bar with a white poodle on her lap. She had on a red wig that was very obvious.

I went up to the bar and asked the bartender if he spoke English. *"Ja, ja,"* he said. "Oh yes. Certainly."

"Then could you tell me where I am?"

"Where you are?" he said. "Why, in Zurich."

"No, no. I mean, what is this neighborhood?"

"The Neiderdorf, of course."

I tried to remember what my guidebook had said about the Neiderdorf. Something about it being Zurich's bohemian district. Something about the fact that tourists shouldn't go there alone.

I ordered a beer and tried to calm my nerves. Then, because I still felt jittery, I asked the lady next to me—the one in the red wig—for a cigaret. She nodded and offered me a Marlboro. I was just about to light it when someone on my left struck a match and said, "Permit me."

It was the man in the leather coat.

He had sat down next to me, and after he lit my cigaret, he ordered a brandy. And to say that I was frightened, Dr. Gutman, is like saying that the Empire State Building is rather tall. I was not just frightened, I was terrified.

He took a sip of his brandy and gave me a little smile. "Herr Chesterfield," he said, "you have led us a merry chase."

I swallowed hard. "I have?"

"Ja, ja, my friend. A merry chase for several days now. Your very good friends . . . they do not know what to make of your behavior."

"Well," I said, "I'm sorry."

"These friends—they think that perhaps you are having a little fun with them. Because they know, of course, that there is no one by the name of Rick Olsen in your hotel room. And that you have not been to Lugano. They think . . . or, I should say, they *hope* you have been playing pranks."

"Well . . ."

Herr Gessner sighed and took another sip of

brandy, and in those few seconds I had a chance to study him. He was a mild-looking person with fat red cheeks and effeminate hands. Small hands. The brown leather coat and brown beret looked sort of foolish on him.

He gazed at me. "You know, of course, that I am Ulrich Gessner?"

"Uh, yes."

"And that I am to give you your instructions?"

I nodded as though I knew exactly what he meant. "Right."

"Well then, let us assume that all the merry pranks are over. And that we are now ready to . . . how do you Americans say it, get down to work? Yes, ready to get down to work."

I ordered another beer and tried to act casual. But privately I was cursing B.C. for getting me into such a crazy situation. What kind of friends did he have, anyway? Lunatics.

"So," said Gessner, "it is this way. Your fur boots will be ready for you this afternoon at four, at Teddy's Boot Shop on the Limmatquai. They are size nine and I am sure will fit you."

"My fur *boots*?"

"*Ja, ja,*" said Gessner, handing me a ticket with

61

some numbers on it. "This ticket will secure them for you."

"Did you really say boots?"

"Of course, my dear Chesterfield. Black sealskin boots. Your very good friends wish to make you a present of them."

"Well . . . that's very nice of them."

Gessner patted his lips with his handkerchief. "Terrible drinks they have here. The brandy will probably give me, how do you say it, a burn of the heart."

"Heartburn. We call it heartburn."

He laughed. "Yes. Well, now I must be going, my dear fellow. And may I wish you a pleasant flight back to New York?"

"Certainly," I said, feeling very relieved. Because it was obvious that this man was not a threat to me. He simply wanted to give me a present of some boots. Mrs. Mendelsohn was right about the Swiss. They were odd.

I spent the rest of the day sitting on some stone steps by the river, feeding the swans, and at exactly four o'clock I went looking for Teddy's Boot Shop on the Limmatquai. It was easy to find because it had a big sign in the window. "Teddy's Booterie," said the sign. "Excellence in shoes."

Teddy himself waited on me—a big, jovial person who spoke English—and when I gave him my ticket, he said, "*Ja, ja,* young man. The black fur boots. Right away."

Well, Dr. Gutman, even *I* was impressed with the boots he brought out from the back of the shop. They were made of black sealskin, and zipped up the front, and had thick crepe soles. They fit me perfectly.

Before I could ask Teddy if the boots were really a present—from my very good friends—he said, "There is no charge for these. The charge has been taken care of. Wear them in health."

The boots looked wonderful on me. I mean, I had seen other guys wearing boots like these in Zurich, so I assumed that they were fashionable. And they were warm, too. Carrying my old shoes in the shopping bag Teddy had given me, I wandered over to the Odeon Cafe for a sandwich—and sat there, wearing my new boots and thinking about Mrs. Mendelsohn. I would spend the next few days sightseeing and learning German, and by the time she

returned from Lugano, I would be *Zurichoise*—
which is a word that Marie, at the desk, uses all
the time. As far as I can tell, it means someone who
is completely at home in Zurich.

That night I dreamed that Mrs. Mendelsohn and
I were on a 747, heading for Lisbon. The plane was
completely empty, except for us, and we were
drinking champagne together and having a wonderful time. Then a stewardess came up to us and
said, "The pilot has just had a heart attack." What
about the co-pilot? I asked her. What about the
navigator? "They have had heart attacks, too," she
replied. Mrs. Mendelsohn looked at me—a long,
erotic look. "My dear," she said, "now is the time
for courage. It is *you* who will fly this plane to
Lisbon."

She embraced me, and I embraced her back, and
then I headed up the aisle towards the cockpit. At
that point, the dream ended.

It's odd, Dr. Gutman, but all the next day I had
the feeling that Ulrich Gessner was following me.
I'd turn around suddenly, on the Limmatquai, only
to think I had seen him darting into the Water
Chapel. I'd be browsing in the crafts shop, when
I'd notice the back of a man in a leather coat heading

out the front door. Then, on the Bahnhofstrasse, I was sure I had seen him stopping to light a cigaret in the doorway of a bank. I was window-shopping on the Bahnhofstrasse because I wanted to buy Mrs. Mendelsohn a present for her return to Zurich. A beautiful handkerchief, perhaps, or a fancy box of chocolates.

Look, I said to myself, Herr Gessner *lives* in Zurich, so it's likely that you have seen him today. Zurich is a very small city. He is probably out shopping too.

And that was when the girl ran into me.

I was standing outside of Sprungli's, looking at a display of chocolates in the window, when this little girl—sprinting along the sidewalk—crashed into me. The same girl I had met in the railway station. She crashed into me, almost knocked me down, recognized me, and said, "Mister, please. *Die Polizei!*"

"What?" I said. But before I could speak further, she had grabbed my hand and was pulling me along with her. Soon we were both running up the Bahnhofstrasse, towards Burkliplatz, as she kept gasping something about the police and the Globus department store. There was almost no way I could understand her rapid German, but I was beginning to get the idea that the cops were after her. And now, of course, they were after me too.

At Burkliplatz, where the sightseeing boats dock, we stopped to catch our breath. "What *is* it?" I said to her. "Are the cops after you?"

"*Ja, ja,*" she gasped. *"Wo wohnen Sie?"*

This time, I understood her. "At the Hotel Opera," I replied. "But . . ."

I never finished the sentence. Once again we were running, and the direction we were running in was my hotel. I looked behind us and could not see any cops, but I ran anyway. Then I saw the sweaters that this kid had stuffed into the front of her army jacket. She had been shoplifting.

Well, the last thing I wanted to do was to enter my hotel with a child shoplifter. Marie, at the desk, would probably think I had lost my mind—but there was no time to consider all this. Running more slowly now, the girl and I went the whole length of the Utoquai, crossed two streets, and plunged into the Hotel Opera. Marie, thank goodness, was nowhere to be seen.

We hurried into the tiny elevator, sailed up to my

66

room, and the minute we were inside I locked the door behind us. "Now look . . ." I began.

The girl threw herself down on one of the twin beds and let out a groan. "Wow!" she said, in her heavy accent. *"Gott!"*

She pulled the stolen sweaters out of her beat-up army jacket, and lay back on the bed. *"Gott,"* she said again.

I was sitting on the other bed, trying to get my breath. "You must be crazy," I said.

She was lying flat, with her eyes closed—and her dirty boots were on my clean white bedspread. She really was a mess—orange crew cut, dirty jeans, three cotton scarves wound around her neck. A Swiss hippie.

I decided to speak to her in German, and tried to think of an appropriate phrase from my phrase book. *"Darf ich mich vorstellen?"* I said. Which means "May I introduce myself?"

The girl opened her eyes, gave me a bored look, and said, "Oh, for God's sake, cut the crap. I'm an American."

You could have knocked me over with a feather. Because of all the things that had happened to me in the past few days, this one was the most surprising. "You're an *American*?" I said.

She took out a bent cigaret from the pocket of her jeans, lit it, and blew the smoke straight up into the air. "That's right, buster. An American. Just like you."

"What makes you think I'm an American?"

At this, she began to laugh.

"What were you doing back there on the Bahnhofstrasse?" I asked her. "Shoplifting?"

"Right. Shoplifting from the Globus department store. But some shit caught me and phoned for the cops. I got away just before they arrived."

Her language startled me. Because she looked around twelve years old. And small even for twelve. "How old are you?" I asked.

"Sixteen. Do I look it?"

"No. You look twelve."

"At times, that can be an advantage."

"How come you're pretending to be Swiss?"

She stared at me. "How come *you* are?"

"Well . . . it's a long story."

She didn't say anything after that—just lay there with her dirty boots on my bedspread, smoking.

After she spilled some ash on the carpet, I went into the bathroom to get an ashtray.

"Would you like something to drink?" I asked, gesturing towards the snack bar.

She propped the pillows behind her and sat up a little. "Hard or soft?"

"Soft."

"No thanks. You wouldn't have any grass, would you? Weed? Maryjane?"

"No. Of course not."

She was looking at me with a look that I can only call contemptuous. "You talk like a faggot. Are you aware of that?"

"No," I said coldly. I sat down in an armchair and opened a can of Coke. "What's your name?"

"Polo Quinn. What's yours?"

"Uh, Brian Chesterfield."

"I bet you're from New York. You have that look."

"What look?"

"That certain look. Paranoid. You live in Manhattan?"

"Queens."

"I live on Sixty-first Street. When I'm in the States,

that is. Do you have anything to eat here? I'm starved."

"Just some peanuts and crackers. In the snack bar."

"Well, hand them *over*, Maurice. I'm on my last legs."

Dr. Gutman, I must make it clear to you that I did not like this girl at all. Outside of the fact that she was dirty and foulmouthed, she was taking over my hotel room like an invading army. After she had eaten all the peanuts and crackers, she drank a fruit drink, combed her hair, and announced that she wanted to take a bath. And because there is a terrible streak of cowardice in me, where women are concerned, I let her. I did not want this girl to use my beautiful red-and-white futuristic bathroom, but could not bring myself to say no.

She ran a hot bubble bath, undressed, and got into the tub without even closing the door. I sat by the window of my room, looking out at Lake Zurich and making firm plans to get rid of this person. I did not give a damn whether the cops were after her or not. The minute she emerged from that tub, I would throw her out.

Well, I didn't. Throw her out, I mean. Because

70

she caught me off guard by coming out of the bathroom with a big white towel wrapped around her, and announcing that she needed to get some sleep.

"Now just hold on . . ." I began. But she was already rolled up in one of the down comforters, and in about two minutes she was snoring. She sounded like J. M. Barrie, one of our cats, who snores very loudly.

It was around five in the afternoon, and I didn't know whether to stay in the room with her, go out for the evening, or bring in some food for both of us. I was worried that Marie, at the desk, would learn that there was a girl in my room and get an entirely wrong impression. So finally I went down to a little restaurant around the corner and bought some sandwiches and cake. As I write this, the girl is still sleeping and I have just finished dinner. Lights are beginning to come on across the lake and the evening is peaceful. When you come right down to it . . .

March 6 Something alarming has happened, and I

71

am on a train heading up into the Swiss Alps. The girl is with me. More later.

March 7 I am in a town called Davos, high in the Alps, about three hours from Zurich. Polo is still with me. She says I will be safe here.

March 8 Dr. Gutman, I keep asking myself, if I had this whole thing to do over again, would I? Because I am now a hunted man, a fugitive, and that was not exactly my purpose in coming to Europe.

I am so angry at B.C. that I could kill him. I don't care if he *is* lying in a hospital somewhere, paralyzed, worrying about his luggage and his black purse. He should never have got me into this mess.

On the other hand, this town is fantastic. An international ski resort! And every single person you see looks like a movie star. If I weren't still so apprehensive, I could be happy here forever—strolling up and down the beautiful main street and having tea every day at Frau Schneider's, which is a terrific pastry shop and restaurant.

I am staying in a hotel called the Europa. The proprietor is a nosy woman named Madame Rudolph.

However. To go back two days . . . The girl slept, I finished my dinner, and wrote a long entry in this notebook. The lights were coming on across Lake Zurich, and the evening was a chalky blue. At six o'clock, church bells began to ring—in Zurich, there are always bells ringing—and as I stared out at the blue evening I felt almost tranquil.

There was a knock at the door.

I glanced at Polo, but the knock didn't wake her, so I went over to the door and opened it. There stood Ulrich Gessner and another man. A man in a raincoat. "Well, hello," I said.

Ulrich Gessner gave me a hard look. "Chesterfield, this is my associate Hans Kubli. We would like to speak with you."

"I'm sorry," I said. "I'm busy at the moment."

Gessner laughed—a laugh that was more like a snort. "Indeed, you have been busy, Herr Chesterfield. *Too* busy, in our opinion."

I glanced at the man in the raincoat, and saw that

his hand was in his pocket. A gun? No, I said to myself, stay calm. It is *not* a gun.

"What is the reason for the change in your schedule?" Gessner asked me. "Speak!"

The man in the raincoat started to push past me, into the room, but then he saw Polo in the bed. *"Ein Augenblick, bitte,"* he said. *"Was ist das?"*

"A guest," I said. "I have a guest."

Ulrich Gessner glanced into the room too, and frowned. "So, Chesterfield, you choose to entertain yourself in Zurich. Very unwise. We will speak downstairs in the lobby then. You will come downstairs."

The man in the raincoat gripped the thing in his pocket a little more tightly. Yes. It was a gun.

"Uh, just give me two minutes," I said to Gessner. "I have to speak to my . . . girlfriend."

"Girlfriend? More likely a whore from the Neiderdorf."

"Right. But I haven't paid her yet and . . ."

Gessner snorted. "You stupid Americans. Don't you know that pleasure and business do not mix?"

The two men looked at each other, and finally the one called Kubli nodded and spoke rapidly to Gessner in Swiss German.

"My associate says that there is no back entrance to this hotel," said Gessner. "So, my dear fellow, there is no chance of your disappearing. We will expect you downstairs."

The minute they were gone, I went over and shook Polo violently. "Wake up!" I said. "Oh God, please wake up. Something has happened!"

She woke instantly, and sat up. "What is it?"

"I'm in trouble. Some men are after me. We have to get out of here."

To my amazement, she leapt into action. I mean, any other girl would have wanted a full explanation, but this character just threw off the bath towel and reached for her clothes. I was so undone that I didn't even mind her nakedness—because I was throwing my possessions into B.C.'s suitcase.

I raced into the bathroom for my toothbrush and my Colgate. My shaving kit. "There are two men waiting for me in the lobby," I said to Polo. "How do we get out of here? There's no back entrance."

"Simple," she said calmly. "We jump."

"*What?*"

"We're only on the second floor, Oliver. So we climb out on that little balcony you have there, and jump."

75

"OK," I said.

We climbed out on the tiny balcony outside my room. Polo took my suitcase, threw it to the street, and then she jumped. I climbed over the balcony railing and looked down. It looked very far. "Jump!" she called to me, so I did. But when I landed, I hurt my ankle.

Polo hailed a cab that was pulling away from the hotel, and pushed me and my suitcase into it. *"Der Hauptbahnhof,"* she said to the driver. "Fast."

I lay back against the seat. "I hurt my ankle. I may have broken it."

"Oh, shit," she said. "Is it swelling up?"

"No. It just hurts."

"We'll take care of it when we get to the railway station. Now look, Fritz, are there really some guys after you—or is this a joke?"

"I *told* you. There are two men after me, and one of them has a gun. I think they want to kill me."

"Jesus. What did you do?"

"I can't talk about it. It's too complicated."

"OK. We'll hide out in the railway station. Listen! We could take a train up to Davos. My father's there."

"Where?"

"Davos. It's about three hours away, in the Alps. They'd never find you."

After a few minutes, she said, "It wouldn't hurt *me* to get out of town, either. I've been robbing this city blind."

Once we were in the railway station—that enormous, echoing place—Polo went over to a lighted sign that kept revolving. It was the timetable of all the trains.

"There isn't a train to Davos until six A.M. So what we do is, we go into a movie and sleep."

"OK."

"How's your ankle? You want me to look at it?"

"No, no. It's better."

We went over to a kiosk and bought food—crackers and apples and chocolate bars—and then we went into a German movie that seemed to be called *My Country Cousin*. And I must say, Dr. Gutman, that it was a very raunchy movie.

The film ran all night, and we stayed there all night, alternately sleeping and eating, and watching a huge blond woman make love to a small blond man. Normally, I would have been horrified to see a film like that with a girl, but all I could think of was that train to Davos.

It wasn't until the train pulled out of the station at six A.M. that I breathed a sigh of relief. Polo had gone very quiet and was staring out of the train window, so I did too. I wondered why her father was up in Davos, and if he was as poor as she was.

Beyond the train window, the suburbs of Zurich were rolling by, with the lake on our left. Stores, parks, apartment buildings—and everyone's clothes hung out on the little balconies. To *air*, I said to myself, that's why they hang them out. The Swiss are so thrifty. They probably don't rush to the dry cleaner every week, like we do.

Then I realized that I hadn't paid my hotel bill, at the Opera. What a thing to do to Marie! I would send her some money from Davos.

"You know," I said to Polo. "I just realized . . ."

I left the sentence unfinished. Because all of a sudden there were the Alps, rising out of the morning mist! They were suddenly just there—like some child's drawing of mountains. Straight up and down.

The train rose steadily into the mountains, passing small clustered villages and old farm buildings—and in every village, no matter how small, there was a church with a beautiful steeple. Everything was covered with snow now, a world of snow.

"This scenery is fantastic," I said to Polo. "But where are the cows?"

She turned and gave me a bored look. "The what?"

"The cows. I thought that Swiss farms had cows."

"They're in the *barns*, Geraldo. They don't come out until spring."

"Why are you calling me Geraldo?" I said. "Or, for that matter, Fritz, Oliver, and Maurice? My name is Brian."

"A private joke. Forget it."

The train climbed higher, and I sat there with my nose pressed to the window. The scenery was like something out of *Heidi*, or maybe *The Sound of Music*. Wooden houses with balconies and sloping roofs. Enormous barns. A cat sitting in the window of an old inn. Two kids pulling a wooden cart through the snow.

An hour passed, then two, and Polo was still quiet. But eventually she said, "We have to change trains in a few minutes. At Landquart."

Which we did—running down a long ramp, and

up onto another platform. This time, our train was bright red and very small. "*Now* the scenery begins," said Polo. "So get out your camera, Maurice."

The train was chugging straight up into the Alps, and the valleys and gorges beneath us took my breath away. "That's Klosters down there," Polo said, pointing to a distant town—and my heart beat fast for a moment. Klosters was where Mrs. Mendelsohn had her weekend house.

As the train pulled into Davos, it began to snow. And as we emerged onto the platform I felt that I had stepped into another world. How beautiful this was! How . . . Swiss. "This is Davos-Dorf," said Polo. "The other end of the town is called Davos-Platz. My dad lives in the middle, above the Promenade."

She hailed a cab, making me wonder how she could afford it. Polo was the poorest person I had met in Switzerland, yet she had a lot of cash on her. Stolen, perhaps. "Does your father expect you?" I asked.

She settled back against the seat of the cab. "No, Clive, he does not expect me. And when he sees me, he will not be thrilled."

"Really? How come?"

"As you would say—a long story. Look. You want to tell me what kind of trouble you're in? It might make things easier."

"Later. Give me time."

Polo pulled a crushed-looking cigaret out of her jeans, and lit it. "You want one?"

"No thanks. I've been smoking ever since I came here, and I don't even like to smoke."

"Are you in Europe because of some broad? Is that it?"

I felt my face turning red. "Well . . . in a way. The thing is—she's older than I am. An older woman."

"No kidding?"

"Her name is Melina and she has grown children and everything. She was once an opera star."

I glanced at Polo, to see if she believed me. It was possible that she did.

"*I* had an affair with a guy forty years old last year," she announced. "The same age as my father."

I didn't want her to see how startled I was by this remark, so I stared out the window of the cab. People in bright ski clothes and molded plastic boots were clop-clopping along the sidewalk.

The next thing that happened was a shock. Because our cab did not pull up in front of a small hotel, or a modest little apartment house. It pulled up in front of something so large that you could only call it a villa. A huge white stucco house, with wooden trim, many balconies, and a glassed-in porch on the top floor. "Is *this* where your dad lives?" I said. Then it occurred to me that he might be a butler or something. A valet.

"This is it," said Polo, paying the cab driver. "The old homestead. In winter, that is. In spring we go to New York. In autumn we head for France."

"God," I said, as we stood looking up at the house. "What business is your father in?"

"He's a writer. Christopher Quinn."

Well, that was my second shock—because Christopher Quinn is a famous writer of suspense novels, and I had read quite a few of them. I liked him almost as well as Ian Fleming, the guy who created James Bond, because Quinn's books were filled with spies and intrigue and lost, beautiful women. Not the sexy women of the Bond stories, but women

82

who looked like wounded deer, and who always came to a bad end.

"I don't get it, Polo. If your dad is Christopher Quinn, then why are you living like a hippie?"

"The word hippie went out long ago," she declared.

"Street person, then! Why are you living like a street person?"

"Because it amuses me. Come on—let's go and meet the genius."

Polo opened the front door with her key—and as we began to climb a long, curving staircase, I tried to remember the last Quinn thriller I had read. It was called *Gardens of Glass* and concerned a young woman being held prisoner in a Long Island mansion where the gardens are creepy and overgrown. The man holding her captive is using hypnosis to try and make her reveal the location of some treasure that was buried in the gardens long ago. By her grandmother. Etc.

We went up two stories. As we approached the third, a man stepped out on the landing and looked down at us. It was Christopher Quinn.

Tall. Blond. Horn-rimmed glasses. Tweed slacks

and a cashmere sweater. It was amazing—he looked exactly the way a famous writer should look. When he saw Polo, he frowned. "What are *you* doing here?" he said.

"Came up for the weekend," she replied. "With my friend Brian."

"What's the matter?" said Mr. Quinn. "Have you run out of stores to rob? Or did you simply run out of marijuana?"

A look of pain crossed Polo's face. "I just came up for the weekend, Daddy. This is Brian."

Quinn didn't even acknowledge me. "I'm working. You know I work in the mornings."

Polo's face had fallen about a mile. "OK. We'll go out for breakfast or something."

"Before you do, I want a word with you. The young man can wait in the library."

Polo disappeared down the hallway with her father, and I went into the library. It was a large room lined with books, and filled with tables and comfortable chairs.

On a round marble table were some framed photos. Christopher Quinn with his arm around a tall, glamorous woman. Polo as a child, in riding clothes. A picture of two dachshunds.

84

Down the hall, I could hear an argument going on. Quinn's voice was raised, and Polo was shouting, "It isn't fair! All I'm asking you is . . ."

She came into the library and slammed the door behind her. "He says you can't stay here. I thought I'd save you the price of a hotel, but the genius is simply too involved in his work. So I'll get you a room at the Europa or something. Jesus. He's so damn mean."

"Does . . . your mother live here too?" I asked.

"My mother's dead."

"Mine too."

Our eyes met for a moment, and then she looked away. "Let's go have breakfast, Oliver. Then we'll hunt for a room."

March 9 I wrote a letter to my father last night, Dr. Gutman. Which was not easy, because I had to leave out most of the things that have happened to me thus far. I mean, can you see me telling my father that I am hiding out in the Swiss Alps because two thugs are after me? Or that my only friend here is a teenage girl who has been smoking joints since she was a child, and who has had around fifty lovers? Because, of course, that's who Fritz, Oliver and Maurice are. Her ex-lovers.

So what I said was that I was having a little holiday in a Swiss mountain resort, and had met some charming people. I told him all about Frau Schneider's restaurant, and the huge modern sports arena. I told him about the pampered Swiss dogs you see trotting along with their masters, and about the terrific-looking people in ski clothes.

I guess I was homesick. The letter went on and on.

"Please don't worry about me," I said in closing, "because I'll be back very soon. Take care of your health, and kiss the cats for me."

The trouble is, I cannot mail this letter from Davos, because a Davos postmark would be dangerous right now. I can just see my father looking at the postmark and racing to Kennedy Airport and flagging down a Swissair jet. No. I will mail it from the anonymity of Zurich—when I return.

It's not that I don't feel safe here, because there is *no way* that Gessner and Kubli can find me in Davos. It's just that this hotel is not at all like the Opera, and that the people are odd. Madame Rudolph, who owns the place, is like an army sergeant.

She sits in the lobby at a card table, with her little dog, drinking beer and commanding her troops— the maids, the kitchen help, Hugo at the desk. She is wildly nosy, and said to me when I checked in, "You have friends in Davos? You are here to ski? You have been to Switzerland before?"

Every few minutes, Madame Rudolph leaves the card table and bustles into the kitchen, to shout orders in various languages. Her daughter (I think it's her daughter) wears a white coat, rather like a dentist, and stands in the small lobby nodding and bowing.

Polo was able to get me a room here because she knows Hugo, the desk clerk. The thing is, she bribed him to register me under a false name—which is illegal. ("I slipped him a few francs to register you under the name of Aldous Huxley," she said to me. "Just to be safe.")

My hotel room is tiny and uncomfortable, and seems to have no heat. The sink is in the room, the toilet is across the hall, and the bathtub is unknown.

My first night in this place was terrible. My ankle was still hurting, the mattress was lumpy, and the room was so cold that I could see my breath when I breathed. The Europa does not serve breakfast in the rooms, so I had supplied myself with a thermos of coffee and some rolls. At any rate, I rose at seven, went across the hall to pee, and came back feeling very depressed. Then, Dr. Gutman, I went out onto my little balcony. All the rooms have balconies.

Beyond me, the snowy Alps were shining in the sun—a ring of Alps, with the town nestled beneath them. Bells were ringing, and men were walking along the street looking like they had just stepped out of an old novel. Knee breeches and loden jackets. Alpine hats with feathers in them. Blackbirds were wheeling through the early sunlight and little red funiculars were heading up the mountains.

How beautiful it was! How serene and European. And how lucky I was to be in the midst of it. My father, who is a real romantic, has never even been to Europe—so all of a sudden I felt very grateful.

After we left Polo's house that first day, we took a bus downtown, to Frau Schneider's restaurant, where we had a big breakfast of eggs and bacon, rolls, cheese, and hot chocolate. The food was fantastic, and I dug right into it. But Polo merely picked at hers. She seemed sad.

"Your father is . . . very interesting," I said to her. "Very high-strung."

"He's a bastard," she replied. "I wouldn't have come up here if it weren't for you. Usually, I just hang around Zurich."

I took a sip of the creamy hot chocolate. "Polo," I said, "how come you're not in school?"

She gave me a sharp look. "How come *you're* not?"

"It's a long story."

"Well, mine isn't a long story. I'm not in school because after my mother died I ran away from three different boarding schools. So my old man decided that tutors would be the thing—except that they're always quitting. They tell him I'm incorrigible."

"Well, aren't you?"

"Sure. Why not? No one in this world gives a damn about me, so why shouldn't I do what I want? In Zurich, I hang around with the street people. In Cannes, I fool around with the rich kids—the ones whose fathers are movie producers or tycoons. When we're in Venice—which we are sometimes— I simply prowl. Like one of the local cats."

"But why does he move around so much?"

"His work. He says that change and variety help him to write those lousy thrillers. We even spent a summer once in Dubrovnik. He was using it as background material."

"When did your mother die?"

"A few years ago. She had cancer."

"Were you close to her?"

"None of your goddam business. Anyway, *he* forgot her in about two minutes, and took up with this fashion model named Topaz. That's her photo in our library. She's about six feet tall and oozes sex appeal. She's on a shoot right now, in Spain."

"It must be hard. Not having a permanent home."

She shrugged. "Who cares? All I'm interested in is living my own life, my own way. If *he* had his way, I'd be growing up in a French convent. While he screws fashion models."

For the rest of the morning, Polo showed me around Davos—the shops and restaurants, the famous church with its twisted steeple, the huge skating rink. She also took me to Migros, which is a variety store, to buy some ski pants. "You'll look funny here if you don't wear ski clothes," she said. "I mean, your boots are all right, but you need some pants and maybe a jacket. When in Rome, do as the Romans do."

"What about you?"

"Oh, *me*. I've got plenty of clothes back at the old homestead. These rags are for Zurich only."

I stopped in the middle of the crowded, noisy store, and said, "Why did you try to beg from me in the railway station that day? You had plenty of cash."

Polo grinned. "As my friend Clive would say, 'A lark, simply a lark.' Clive is English."

"Who is Clive, Polo? And who are Fritz, Oliver and Maurice? Who is Geraldo?"

"Men I have laid. Or, as you would say, ex-*lovers*. Really, Fritz, you must stop talking in that sissy way. It will get you in trouble."

As we walked back up the Promenade, lugging my suitcase, Polo explained that it was going to be hard to find me a room because it was still "the season." But we did—and that was when she bribed Hugo.

A word about Hugo. He is around twenty, Italian, handsome in a tough-looking way—and he has a thing about Polo. I can't imagine why because she is not exactly feminine. But Polo says that he is saving money to go to Hollywood, to break into the movies, and that he is convinced she and her father can help him. "He's crazy for anything American," said Polo. "He'll talk your ears off."

Have to stop writing. Polo is at the door.

<u>March 10</u> Yesterday I went up to the Parsenn with Polo and her father—and it was one of the most tremendous experiences of my life. The Parsenn is that mountain B.C. told me he was going to ski on— though of course it is now obvious that *that* was not his purpose in coming to Europe. The more I think about it, the more I suspect that B.C. is heavily in debt to Gessner and Kubli. Maybe an unpaid business loan. Maybe some business venture gone bust. Anyway, Polo surprised me yesterday by appearing at my door dressed in ski clothes, and announcing that she and her father were going to take me up to the Parsenn. "Your father's coming too?" I asked in surprise. "Right," she said. "He wants to check you out."

She sat on my bed while I changed into my new ski pants and jacket. "What does he want to check out?" I asked.

92

"Oh, I don't know. Whether you deal, or something like that. Whether you're a hood. He thinks that all of my friends are hoods."

Mr. Quinn was sitting on a bench in the lobby reading a magazine. He rose as we stepped out of the elevator, and I saw that he looked very glamorous. Black boots, black ski pants, a heavy sweater and a suede jacket. Dark glasses. He gave me a cool look. "Brian, is it?"

"Uh, yes sir," I said. "Brian Chesterfield. From New York."

We shook hands, and it was obvious that he intended to be friendlier than he had been the other day. The three of us headed for the front door, but were stopped by Madame Rudolph. "You are going skiing, young man?" she asked me. "You will be away for the afternoon?"

Praying that she would not call me by my new name—Huxley—I nodded yes and tried to walk past her. "Which mountain do you ski?" she demanded. "The weather is ominous."

"The Parsenn," I replied. "But the weather is fine. Really."

She put one hand to her forehead. "The Parsenn! A place of broken bones. My cousin broke his leg

93

on the Parsenn. A rescue team had to liberate him."

As we rode uptown on the local bus, I kept glancing at Christopher Quinn, trying to size him up. He was a very angry person—even when he was trying to be pleasant—and I had the feeling that he was filled with resentments against Polo. I wondered if he really cared what she did, or whether he was simply concerned about his image. His clothes, and well-cut blond hair, and dark glasses, told me that image was a very big thing to him.

A half hour later we were on a funicular, going up a mountainside. And as the town of Davos fell away beneath us, I saw—for the first time—the majesty and grandeur of the Alps. The town just got smaller and smaller as the mountains loomed up like gods.

We landed at the first station of the Parsenn, and I was absolutely dumbstruck at seeing the world from such a height—a geography of mountain peaks under a brilliant sky. There was a narrow terrace with deck chairs, and a restaurant. Skiers were darting down the slopes like colored dragonflies. "We'll have coffee here," said Mr. Quinn. "Or chocolate. Whichever you kids prefer."

Polo went off to the bathroom, and Quinn and I

got mugs of hot chocolate and settled down in chairs on the terrace. "You ski?" he asked me.

"Uh, no sir. Not really."

He took a sip of his chocolate. "Where did you meet Polo?"

"In Zurich. We sort of . . . bumped into each other."

Quinn was sizing me up, the way I had sized *him* up on the bus. I couldn't imagine what he was thinking. "Where do you go to school?" he asked.

I decided to lie my way through this entire interview. "In Manhattan," I said. "A private school called Spencer. We're on spring break right now. Actually, I came over here on a school tour."

"Really?" said Quinn. He had taken off his dark glasses and was staring at me. "Then where's the rest of the tour?"

"Here! Right here in Davos. But we're scattered at the moment—everyone doing his own thing. You know how it is."

It was crazy, but he seemed to believe me. "Is Polo on drugs at the moment? I'm never quite sure."

"Oh, no sir," I assured him. "Absolutely not. She's clear as a bell."

Just beyond us, skiers were whizzing down the

slopes. Some of them had dogs with them, and the dogs were running alongside.

"I've washed my hands of her, you know," said Quinn. "I've given up."

"Oh?" I said politely.

"She wants to run free? Fine. I've done all I can."

I was beginning to wish that Polo would hurry up and join us, because I felt uncomfortable. On the other hand, how many times in life does one get to talk to a famous writer? There were all kinds of things I wanted to ask him, but the opportunity wasn't presenting itself.

"She was arrested for shoplifting last year, did you know that?" said Quinn. "In New York. They took her to the police station."

"Well . . ."

"And the year before that, she told me she was pregnant. Fortunately, it turned out to be a false alarm."

"I see."

"She's had the best that money could buy—counseling, special boarding schools, psychiatry. And what good has it done? Tell me that."

"Here I am!" said Polo, joining us on the terrace.

"Fifteen minutes in line just to take a leak. What a fucking bore."

Christopher Quinn winced. "Here's your hot chocolate," he said.

For the next half hour the three of us rested on the terrace, lying in deck chairs with our faces to the sun. Then Polo announced that she wanted to go to the top of the mountain. "We take a cable car," she said to me. "So I hope you're not afraid of heights."

The top of the Parsenn is eight thousand feet high, Dr. Gutman. Eight thousand. And as the cable car swung us higher and higher, I began to feel euphoric. Then we were stepping out of the car at the top of the mountain, with snow up to our knees and the wind blowing. The sky was so bright I could hardly look at it, and the entire world seemed to have disappeared. The world had turned into an ocean of jagged peaks—white and blue in the sun.

Standing there on the mountaintop, I began to cry. Not in an obvious way, not so anyone would notice, but in a deep and silent way. And do you know why I was crying, Dr. Gutman? Because I wanted my father to see this too. All I could think of was him sitting back there in Queens, correcting exam papers in a roomful of cats. And here *I* was—standing on the top of the world.

We stood there in the wind for a few minutes, and then we took a cable car down, jammed in with a lot of skiers. And though I am not afraid of heights, going down was a lot worse than going up. We simply *dropped* down, vertically, until we were back at the first station.

During this whole adventure, Polo and her father barely talked to each other. He seemed completely alienated from her, and the more alienated he seemed, the more she used four-letter words. And when she ran out of four-letter words, she started telling outrageous stories about things she had done in Zurich. Things so bizarre that I knew she hadn't done them. And why was she acting this way? Merely to get his attention, to make him act like a parent.

But parenting, obviously, was not in Mr. Quinn's repertoire. When we got back to Davos, he bid us good-bye and walked away—down the long main street.

"Well, see you around," said Polo. "I've got to check in with my parole officer."

"What?"

"I thought that would wake you up. You're in some kind of daze."

"The mountain," I said slowly. "Going up the mountain."

"Right—it's a spiritual experience. It can also give you diarrhea."

"I beg your pardon?"

"A lot of people get sick the first time. That's all."

I gazed at her. She seemed so small in her ski clothes. And her orange hair looked worse than ever. "Polo . . . why do you try so hard to shock him?"

"I don't know. It amuses me."

"Well, it may amuse you, but it really turns him off. You want to get his attention, so you act outrageous. But the more outrageous you act, the more you lose him."

"What are you?" she said angrily. "Some kind of psychologist?"

"No. Of course not."

"Some kind of *philosopher*? Well, let me tell you something, Aldous. If I didn't act outrageous, he wouldn't know I was alive. It's the only goddam communication we have."

And with that, she hopped a passing bus and disappeared.

March 11 Sunday. Snow shining on the Alps and the sound of church bells. I got up early, breakfasted, and walked all the way downtown. Everyone was out walking, and the skiers were heading towards the funiculars. Nobody jogs here, like they do in New York—but on the other hand, who needs to jog? The young people ski, the middle-aged do cross-country skiing, and the old promenade.

I walk. The little train from Landquart sounds its high, thin whistle. The church bells peal one note, over and over. The blackbirds wheel and turn. Could I live here forever? Yes. If my father would come twice a year to visit me.

I love the fact that the dogs in Davos go down ski slopes with their masters. And the fact that little kids, no more than four or five, ski down small slopes held between the knees of their parents. I love the fact that in Migros everything is jumbled together—the clothing next to the food, the ski boots next to the cosmetics. Speaking of which, I bought another pair of ski boots, because the boots Gessner gave me are too warm. Polo says that I am finally fitting in with this milieu.

I'm lonely for her today, and don't know why. Because after all, Dr. Gutman, she is not exactly ingratiating. Every time she says fuck I want to wash her mouth out with soap. I had hoped I would see her this afternoon, but she and Quinn are going to lunch down in Klosters with some people named Throckmorton.

I spent the whole day walking.

March 12 This is being written late at night. I am terrified. I have pushed my bureau against the door of my hotel room and have double-locked my balcony door. I am in trouble, real trouble, and it is very possible that I am doomed.

Polo says everything will be OK. But she is not *God*. She is simply a very small girl who likes using four-letter words.

I'll say one thing, though. She's tough.

Who would have thought that what happened today could have happened to us? She and I were simply sitting in Frau Schneider's having lunch. A very good lunch of steak and potatoes, and rolls and butter, and hot chocolate—which I never got to finish—because the man next to me, at the adjoining table, was drumming his fingers on the tablecloth.

The tables at Frau Schneider's are very close together, Dr. Gutman. So the fact that I just happened to glance at the hands of the man at the next table— and noticed that he was drumming his fingers— was not unusual.

But the hands of this man were very small and soft. Almost effeminate.

They were the hands of Ulrich Gessner.

I raised my eyes from his hands and looked at him. He looked back at me. And of course his sidekick, Kubli, was with him. Wearing that raincoat.

It was odd, but for a while we simply looked at each other. Politely. Then each of us returned to what he was eating. "Don't look now," I said to Polo, "but the two thugs are here. From Zurich. At the next table."

"Right," she said, stubbing out her cigaret. I swear to God, she didn't even blink.

"What do we do?" I asked her, trying to calm my heart, which was pounding like a sledgehammer.

"Easy," she said. "We split."

She jumped up from the table and made for the front door.

I followed close behind, but when I looked back I could see that Gessner and Kubli were on their feet too. "You will wait, please!" Gessner called out to me, but it was too late. Polo and I were racing through the door and up the street.

I glanced back and saw that luck was with us. Because, in his haste to follow us, Gessner had knocked down an old woman on the sidewalk. A very old woman. He had no choice but to stop and pick her up. Kubli stopped too.

"Hurry!" Polo shouted. She was running uptown, towards my hotel, and I had no idea what she had in mind. But then she turned back and said, "Listen, Oliver, can you ice-skate?"

"No!" I said.

"Well, you can now. We're going into the ice rink."

Dr. Gutman, this skating rink is an outdoor one, and it is the size of a football field. Out on the ice hundreds of people were skating—and before I knew it, Polo had pulled me into the place, paid our admission, and rented two pairs of skates.

She dragged me out onto the ice.

We began to go round the skating rink with all the others. But I was having trouble keeping my balance. I had only skated once before, in Rockefeller Center, and it had been a disaster. "Aha!" said Polo. "I see two kids I know. We're in luck."

She glided up to two teenagers, spoke rapidly to them in German, and suddenly they were exchanging ski jackets with us. They also gave us their wool caps and their sunglasses. "Put on these things," Polo said to me. "Quick! I told them it's a drug bust and you and I need disguises."

Dragging me with her, Polo worked her way into the heart of the crowd. "At least *pretend* that you can skate!" she said. "Jesus. You're like a sack of potatoes."

I tried. But my ankles were turning in as though I was crippled. I clung to Polo like a life raft.

"There they are!" I said. "Just coming in."

Gessner and Kubli were walking down the ramp towards the ice rink. But when they had last seen us, I had been wearing a black ski jacket and Polo

104

a white one. Now we were dressed in red and blue.
Plus wool caps and sunglasses. The two men stood
at the edge of the crowd, studying it. Gessner had
binoculars.

"He's got binoculars!" I said to Polo.

"Never mind. Just keep on skating."

We must have gone around that rink for a solid
hour—Polo with her arm around my waist, and me
with my ankles caving in. My right ankle still hadn't
recovered from that jump out of the Hotel Opera,
and now I was skating on it.

Finally—finally!—the two men left. And as soon
as they did, Polo returned our disguises to their
original owners. With me limping, we went into the
restaurant of the ice rink. "I need a brandy," she
said. "What about you, Geraldo?"

"Fine," I replied. I was trembling.

We each had a brandy. And for a long while we
didn't speak. Then Polo said, "All right, Fritz. It's
time for you to tell me the truth. What's going on?"

So I told her everything—and it was such a relief
to be sharing my story with someone that I just
couldn't stop talking. I talked for twenty minutes.
A half hour. At last, I ran out of breath.

Polo was staring at me. "You know something,

105

kid? The story you have just told me is so bizarre that it's probably true. I mean, who could make up such a thing? Coming to Zurich by accident. Using another guy's passport. It's bizarre."

"Right."

"Why did you get on the plane in the first place? You didn't have to."

I searched for the appropriate words. "Because . . . I have never been anywhere in my life. Because I wanted adventure."

"My mom used to say, Beware of what you wish for, because it might happen. But to get back to Gessner. Are you sure he chased you all over Zurich just to give you a present?"

"Yes. All he wanted was to give me those boots. But then he showed up at the door of the hotel room while you were sleeping. And I'm certain the other guy had a gun."

"It's probably some dispute over a woman."

"I don't think so. I think it's some kind of business deal gone bust."

She shook her head. "Nope, it's a broad. The only things that make men go crazy are money and broads. And I don't think it's money. Maybe your pal B.C. stole Gessner's wife or something. Maybe they were sharing the same mistress without knowing it. That happened to my dad just before he met Topaz. He was seeing some actress in Zurich who was also seeing a banker. He went crazy when he found out."

"What I don't understand is how those two characters found me here. It doesn't make sense."

Polo thought for a moment. "Have you been in contact with anyone in Zurich?"

"No. Just Marie, at the desk of the hotel. I sent her some francs to cover my bill."

"Well, that's the answer, Aldous! Your letter had a postmark on it, and the postmark said Davos. All those guys had to do was ask if she'd heard from you."

My heart sank. "Right. That was probably what happened."

"So where do we go from here?"

"I'm going to have to leave, that's all. Go back to Zurich and get a plane to New York. Those guys want to kill me."

"You go to Zurich—they'll follow. You get on the plane to the States, they will too. Nope. What I think we should do is confront them."

"What?"

"You've never even asked them what they want. I mean, maybe it's something very simple."

"I'm not that brave."

"Balls. Of course you are. You got yourself this far, didn't you? From Queens, New York, to the Alps. We'll just walk up to them and ask. First, however, we'll have to find out where they're staying."

Can't write anymore. Too sleepy. Have got to sleep.

March 14 We can't find them. It's crazy, but we can't. Polo checked all the hotels in Davos, and they're not registered. Meanwhile, I have not left the Europa, because I'm scared to bump into them. I've taken asylum here, so to speak, eating all my meals in the restaurant downstairs, prowling the lobby, leafing through Madame Rudolph's dog-eared magazines. This woman has been driving me insane with her questions. ("You are not going skiing today? Where is your friend with the orange hair? You will be taking your meals with us now?") and her daughter keeps hovering around me as though I was ill and needed medical care. Nevertheless. I do not want to leave this hotel until Polo locates the two thugs.

Hugo, whose English is pretty good, has gotten the idea that because I'm American, I know a lot of movie stars. "You know Cher?" he asked me this morning. "You know, perhaps, Sylvester Stallone?" No, I said, no. I don't know anyone. I live in New York. "But many films are reproduced in New York, are they not?" he said. Produced, I corrected him. Look—I don't know anything. I'm not in the movie business.

"You have met, perhaps, Woody Allen?" Hugo said hopefully. "Carol Burnett?"

"No!" I shouted. Which seemed to hurt his feelings.

"*Signore,*" he said to me, "there is no reason for you to become frantic. I only ask who you know in America. If I offend, you must forgive me."

It's six in the evening, and Polo has been gone since noon. Wait! She's here. She's found them.

March 15 Ten P.M. Am writing this at Polo's house,

because she thinks it is no longer safe for me at the hotel. She convinced her father to let me stay here for a while, because she said that my room at the Europa had no heat and I was coming down with a cold. Which is true. I have a cold, my ankle is still hurting, and I want to go home. Yes, home. To Queens, New York, and my father, and the cats. I can't help it. I'm just not as brave as Polo—who is so daring that she should probably become a bull-fighter or a test pilot. Or a Green Beret, except that I don't think they take women.

We confronted them today. Up at the Hotel Schatzalp. Polo never thought of looking for them there.

She had checked every hotel in Davos without thinking of the Schatzalp, because it is so fancy— a place that was once a TB sanatorium for the kings and queens of Europe. But finally she found that they were registered there—Gessner and Kubli—so we decided to take the little blue funicular up to the hotel. And because it was Hugo's day off, she persuaded him to come with us as a bodyguard. She didn't tell him why we needed a bodyguard, but he agreed anyway. Hugo is not too bright.

It takes the funicular four minutes to reach the hotel. And then you are simply *there*—in the midst of a movie by Fellini or someone. If I hadn't been so nervous, I would have studied all this old-world opulence. But to tell you the truth, Dr. Gutman, I felt faint.

Maybe it was my cold, or my ankle, or the fact that the rich food here has been making me slightly sick—but as we stepped off the funicular I began to feel dizzy. "It's lunchtime," said Polo. "How much do you want to bet that they're eating on the terrace, at the snow buffet?"

Which is where they were—the snow buffet being a bank of snow on which platters of food are laid out. People help themselves to delicacies and then eat looking out at the view. Quite fantastic.

They were sitting in deck chairs with wine glasses in their hands. Staring at the Alps. Or at least, Gessner was. Kubli was dozing with his face to the sun. "Herr Gessner?" said Polo. "Hi. I'm Polo Quinn."

To say that Gessner went pale as we walked up to him would be an understatement. All the color drained from his face, and he spilled his wine. Abruptly, Kubli woke up. *"Was?"* he said.

111

"Hi," I said. "Nice to see you fellows again. May we join you?"

We all stared at each other—the two thugs looking incredulous, Polo and me trying to look cool, and Hugo trying to look like a bodyguard. He was dressed for the part in tight pants, a black leather jacket, and dark glasses.

Gessner put down his wine glass and rose to his feet. He looked me up and down—from my shoes to the top of my head. He nodded to himself and made a little clucking sound. "So, Mr. Rick Olsen," he declared. "You grow weary of the chase."

"I beg your pardon?" I said.

"Who are these people with you?" Gessner asked.

I decided to take a leap into the unknown. "This young lady is my, uh, fiancée. The gentleman is our bodyguard."

"Bodyguard? You disappoint me, my dear young man. A bodyguard is not needed here. But it is unwise for you to run away each time we try to make contact. It wastes time, and it costs money. Please," he said courteously, "do sit down. You will be my guests for lunch."

Underneath all his smiles, I could see that Gessner was agitated. There was a vein throbbing in his forehead, and he was sweating.

The waiter brought us all glasses of wine. Polo lit a cigaret and smiled at everyone. Hugo—enjoying his role as bodyguard—sat close to me, a scowl on his face.

There was silence for a while. Then Gessner took me to one side, a few feet away from the others. "Olsen, I am going to speak bluntly. The people in charge are well aware now that you have taken Chesterfield's place, and that you spoke the truth when you said, some days ago, that he was in Lugano. So they conclude that either he has turned the operation over to you—or that you have disposed of him."

I choked on my wine. "*Disposed* of him? Brian? No, really, he's fine. Actually . . . he's right here. In Davos."

Gessner looked stunned. "You are jesting."

"No, no, I'm not. We're all here together. On a skiing vacation."

What have you *done*? I said to myself. But it was too late. I couldn't take it back.

"And the goods?" Gessner asked.

"Well . . ."

113

"If, at this point, the goods are not returned, then it goes hard with you, young man. Where is Chesterfield staying?"

"In a private house," I said desperately. "With friends."

"*Ja, ja*. Then tomorrow you will bring him to us. We will, how do you say it, iron the whole thing out. But I tell you one thing, Olsen, never again will the people in charge give assignments to you young people. You are not to be trusted, because always the pleasure comes first. Am I right? You frolic, you ski, you engage in the *après-ski*, and meanwhile the business of the world goes undone."

He took a package of Tums from his jacket and popped two in his mouth. "The whole thing disturbs my stomach," he said. "I have had a sour stomach from the day I met you."

"Look—I'll bring Brian to see you tomorrow, Why don't we all have lunch at Frau Schneider's?"

Out of the corner of my eye I could see that Polo was listening to this conversation. The look on her face was amazing.

"Fine," said Gessner. "Twelve noon at the restaurant."

At that point, Hugo interrupted us. It was clear

114

that he was taking his role of bodyguard very seriously. He swaggered up to us and said something in German to Gessner.

Gessner laughed. Or rather, he snorted. "Your bodyguard tells me that he is armed and that I should not harass you. Harass! As though I intended to, my dear Olsen. Come. Let us have our meal."

To make a long story short, the five of us had lunch—and anyone watching from a distance would have thought that we were simply a group of friends having lunch on a terrace. Gessner laughed and joked, and said pleasant things to Polo—but he also kept popping Tums into his mouth. Beneath his pleasant manner, he was very nervous.

As we rose to say good-bye, he put his arm around my shoulder and lowered his voice. "We meet tomorrow then, at the restaurant. And if there is any—how shall I say—hanky-panky, then we crack down hard. Because the people in charge have come to the end of their patience. One less Rick Olsen in the world is, to them, of no consequence."

Polo, Hugo and I boarded the little blue funicular. The doors closed, and the train began to slide down the track towards Davos. Hugo had taken off his dark glasses and was grinning. "How was it?" he asked us. "Did I seem very much like the bodyguard?"

"Yeah," said Polo bitterly. "You were great."

"Perhaps one day, in films, I will play such a part."

"Right," she said.

The minute we had debarked from the train, Hugo announced that he had a dentist appointment and took off. And it was then that Polo turned her fury on me. "I was listening to the whole thing!" she said. "Why did you say you'd produce Brian Chesterfield? And who the hell is Rick Olsen?"

"He's a kid back home. He goes to my school."

"Fine, great. So let's phone him and have him fly over. Because you have really screwed up this whole situation. How the fuck are we going to produce Brian Chesterfield? Tell me that."

"I wish you wouldn't swear."

"Swear! You're lucky that's all I'm doing. I could kill you for being so stupid. . . . OK, OK. Let me think for a moment."

Polo walked over to a bench near a bus stop and sat down. She pulled out a bent cigaret and lit it.

She stared into the distance. After a few minutes, I sat down with her.

"OK," she said at last. "I've got it. Down in Klosters is this person named Eddie Throckmorton. He's a college dropout, around twenty. Very handsome and very dumb. His parents come here to ski every winter, and this guy *owes me*. I got him out of a fix last year, and he really owes me. So he will be Brian Chesterfield. For a few hours."

"But Polo . . . suppose they kill him?"

"Better him than you," she said. And we started to laugh.

We laughed so hard that several people who were standing at the bus stop turned and looked at us. "Listen," I said to Polo, "all of a sudden, Gessner's talking about some 'goods.' What could they be?"

"I have no idea."

"Well, why doesn't he just come out with it? Everything is so damn oblique."

"Use your head, Oliver! He's not sure who you are. Why would he tell you what the scam is if he thinks you're an imposter?"

"I wonder why they let us get away each time? It's very strange."

She pondered this for a moment. "I think it's a cat and mouse game. They let you go so they can observe you. Because of course you know that we are being observed all the time."

"By Gessner and Kubli?"

"By *many* people," she said ominously. "What I haven't told you, Maurice, is that you and I are being followed all over Davos. And not by Gessner and Kubli. I mean, I've seen at least two other people tailing us. One was a woman."

I put my head in my hands. "Oh, no. It's too much."

"It's a lot," she admitted.

"I better tell them that my name is Archie Smith. The whole thing has gone too far."

Polo gave me one of her bitter smiles. "And what proof do you have that you're Archie Smith? Your I.D. says Brian Chesterfield, and you're registered at the hotel as Aldous Huxley. Meanwhile, you've just assured them that you are Rick Olsen."

"Maybe I should just cut my throat. It would be quicker."

"Nope, it would just be messy. But I do think you better sleep over at my house tonight. It'll be safer."

118

<u>March 16</u> The plan with Throckmorton worked! But Polo and I are preparing to leave Davos, because it's too dangerous for us here. Polo is supposed to start with a new tutor in three days, but she said what the hell, *this* was more important. It's fantastic how loyal this girl is to me, Dr. Gutman. And I don't even know why.

Before I explain how we passed off Eddie Throckmorton as Brian Chesterfield, I want to say something here. Which is that I kissed her last night. Polo. It was the last thing I expected to happen.

She had gotten her father's permission for me to sleep over—and yet the odd thing was that I didn't lay eyes on the man. He stayed in his studio all evening, had the maid bring his dinner in there, and never came out to talk to us. Yes, there are maids here, Dr. Gutman, two of them, and the house is very elegant. Old, dark, polished furniture. Thick rugs.

Polo and I had dinner alone, in the small paneled dining room, and then she said she was going off to soak in a tub because she had gotten chilled up at the Schatzalp. I went to my own room and lay down on the bed, thinking of Mrs. Mendelsohn and wondering where she was. I have been phoning her

ever since I came to Davos—at both her numbers—
but there is never any answer.

I lay there for a while, thinking and dozing, and
then all of a sudden Polo was in the room, her
cheeks flushed from the hot tub, and her hair slicked
back. She was wearing a white terry-cloth bathrobe.

"Are you asleep?" she asked, sitting down on the
side of the bed.

"No. Not yet."

"I was thinking, as I lay in the tub, that what we
should really do is give this whole situation to my
father. He could use it for a thriller."

I smiled at her. "What your mother said was right.
Beware of what you wish for."

"Aldous? Do you think I should let my hair grow
out? I'm tired of orange."

"What color is it really?"

"Blond. I wonder if I'll ever get any taller? I'm
such a runt."

"I like the way you look," I said to her. "You're
pretty."

"*Pretty?* You need glasses."

"Was your mom tall?" I said carefully.

"Yes."

"You must really miss her."

Polo looked away from me. "I do. I think about her all the time. . . . How old were you when yours died?"

"Twelve."

"I was thirteen, and we were living in France. Her name was Jenny. Would you like to see her picture?"

When I nodded, Polo went to her room, and returned with a framed photo. "*He* doesn't keep her picture around anymore because of Topaz, but I do. Here it is."

I sat up on the bed as she handed me a photo in a silver frame. It showed a terrific-looking woman with long blond hair sitting on a horse. She was wearing a tweed jacket and jodhpurs.

"She loved everything to do with horses. That's why she named me Polo."

"She's beautiful."

To my amazement, I saw that there were tears in Polo's eyes. "Right, she really was. And smart, too. And honest. She always leveled with me about everything, and that's very rare for a parent. I mean, most parents will lie about certain things—their relationships, their problems—but my mom never did. She loved me enough to be truthful."

121

I took Polo's hand. "You know, *he* probably loves you too. It's just that your behavior pushes him away."

She shook her head. "Nope. The year before she died, I overheard one of their arguments. And you know something? He shouted at her that he had never wanted a kid in the first place. That she had tricked him into having one."

"Come on. That's just something he said in anger."

"All that man cares about is his work, and his fame, and knowing important people. He's never given a damn about me. But my mom wanted me so much that she lied. What I suspect is that she waited to tell him until it was too late."

"Too late for what?"

"An abortion."

Don't ask me why, Dr. Gutman, but I put my arms around her at that point. "Don't think about it."

"I miss my mother," said Polo.

She was crying—just like a little kid—and the whole thing unnerved me so much that I kissed her. First her cheek, and then, very briefly, her mouth. We clung to each other. "It will be all right," I mumbled. "Things will work out."

"Why do you say that? Almost nothing in this world works out."

"It will be OK."

Then she kissed me, gently, on the mouth—and I became very aroused. "Polo . . ."

She pulled away and looked at me. And suddenly she was different. "So now we make out, right? You and me, here in the guest room. Or would you prefer the library floor? Some people think that floors are sexy."

"But . . ."

"Well, I don't make out anymore, Oscar, so you'd better adjust. I don't roll around in the back of cars, and I don't go to people's hotel rooms, and I don't do it in bathtubs. This woman who used to be my governess, Miss Macy, was right. She said that men only want one thing. She was sixty years old and crazy as a bedbug, but she was right."

She stomped out of my room, slamming the door behind her—and I sat there, bewildered. First because of her behavior, and second because I hadn't even known I was attracted to her. But I was. Wildly, passionately attracted.

I didn't get much sleep that night, knowing that Polo was sleeping in the next room. I kept wondering what it would be like to make love with her, the two of us warm and naked in a single bed. Our arms and legs around each other. Close, close.

Then I thought about my father, and how much I missed him—and how different he was from Polo's father. *I*, at least, had been wanted. And though I've never accomplished a thing in this world, he has always acted like I'm a star. My first poem, written in the third grade, hangs on his bedroom wall in a frame. And there's a photo of me taken during the Eighth Grade Debate hanging in the kitchen. The subject, if I remember it correctly, was, "Does mankind have a future?"

The next morning, Polo was all business. It was as though nothing had happened between us the night before, nothing at all. She had already phoned Eddie Throckmorton, and he had agreed to drive up to Davos and impersonate someone named Brian Chesterfield. "I have a game plan," she said to me, "but I'm not telling you what it is, Fritz. So at the luncheon, just keep your mouth shut."

Eddie Throckmorton was exactly the way Polo had described him. Around twenty, very handsome, and a jerk. When she introduced us in front of the restaurant, he just gave me a weak smile. He seemed a little retarded, but he did have a wonderful car—an Alfa Romeo. Like Polo, he was a rich kid.

Gessner and Kubli were waiting for us at a large table in the rear of the restaurant—and as we approached, they gave each other a significant look, the meaning of which I could not fathom. Then Polo was introducing Eddie as Brian Chesterfield, and Eddie was bowing and nodding. "The only problem is . . ." said Polo, "that Brian's got laryngitis at the moment. He's lost his voice."

Gessner and Kubli glanced at each other.

"However," said Polo brightly, "you can ask him anything you want, and he'll write it down on this pad he brought along. We're really sorry for the inconvenience."

The minute lunch was ordered, Gessner began asking Eddie questions—all of them carefully worded—and Eddie kept replying by scribbling on the white pad. Gessner and Kubli would study the pad, not be able to read Eddie's writing, and ask Polo to translate for them. Polo would stare at the pad for a while, frowning, and then she would say, "Gee, Herr Gessner, I'm not sure. I *think* he has written here that his pig escaped from the farm. No, of course not! That can't be it. The word isn't pig, it's . . . dig. Or maybe, rig. That's it! He wonders why you want the situation rigged."

It got worse and worse. Or—depending on how you look at it—better and better. Gessner was so angry that he was red in the face. And Kubli kept whispering things to him in Swiss German. "This is outrageous!" said Gessner. "I cannot communicate with this person!"

"Herr Gessner," said Polo coolly, "there is no reason to be rude. Brian is *trying* to answer your questions. It isn't his fault if his handwriting is poor."

"But there are certain things I require from this young person! Certain things concerning his . . . schedule."

"Fine," said Polo. "He'll be glad to write down his schedule for you. In detail."

At the exact same moment, Polo and I saw the newcomers.

They were sitting at a table at the other end of the room—a man and a woman dressed in ski clothes—and the man was taking pictures of our group with a very small camera. I looked at Polo and she nodded. They were the two people who had been following us. In their forties, perhaps, and very similar-looking. They could have been twins.

126

None of us had touched our lunch, which I regretted because I was very hungry. But just as I was about to take a mouthful of veal and potatoes, Polo gave me one of her sharper looks. A look that meant, Be prepared, Maurice, something is about to happen.

It did. Because suddenly Hugo (of all people) burst into the restaurant and screamed, "Fire!" He screamed it in three languages, French, German, and English, and within seconds all hell had broken loose. People were racing for the front door, two waiters had spilled trays of food, and a woman sitting next to us with a poodle had become hysterical. Polo pushed our table over on Gessner and Kubli—who disappeared beneath platters of potatoes and veal—and then she and I and Throckmorton split. We made for the side door while everyone else was hurrying towards the front door. I looked back once, and saw that Gessner was just getting to his feet, a piece of veal on his head. We got into Eddie's car and raced away.

"Wasn't Hugo good?" Polo said, as the Alfa Romeo sped up the Promenade.

"You didn't tell me about Hugo," I said to her.

"It was all in the game plan, Maurice."

A few hours later Throckmorton is going to pick us up here at Polo's house at four A.M. Then he will drive us to Zurich. Polo says that he doesn't mind doing this because he has a girlfriend down there, a waitress. His parents don't know about her.

Later still Against Polo's wishes, I went back to the hotel to get the last of my things, and found that my room had been ransacked! I had taken my clothes to Polo's house, and my black purse and money, etc., but I had left a few things behind— all of which they took.

What are they looking for? "The goods." But these goods could be anything. I once knew a kid named Tom Roth, whose father worked in the Garment District in Manhattan, and Tom's father was always referring to ladies' clothes as "the goods." But surely Gessner is not losing his mind over some ladies' clothes. Weird, very weird.

The night clerk was on duty when I went to the hotel, so I left him some money for Madame Rudolph—for the room. My departure will be a mystery to her.

<u>Even later</u> I am packed, and Polo and I are waiting for Throckmorton to arrive. Polo's father is asleep. She has left him a note saying that she'll be back in a few days. She is wearing her Zurich clothes again.

<u>March 18</u> Zurich! How wonderful it looks, even in the rain. The church bells, the somber skies, the swans sailing by on the river . . . all this is familiar now. Under the arcades on the Limmatquai, vendors are selling bunches of spring flowers. There are street musicians playing classical music in St. Peter's Square. And even though Polo and I are sleeping in sleeping bags on the Utoquai, I am happy. Because we are together.

<u>March 19</u> We are both dressed as street people now, my luggage is in a locker at the railway station, and I have met five kids—all acquaintances of Polo's—who are living the same way we are. Sleeping in

parks. Scrounging. The only difference is that Polo and I are not high. Everyone else is stoned.

I begin to think that Polo lies about a lot of things—like smoking grass. Never once have I seen her smoke a joint, and she doesn't seem interested in the harder stuff. The only substance we take is a little wine, when we eat a meal in one of the small restaurants in the Neiderdorf.

Gessner and Kubli would no longer recognize me—I look so shabby. Faded jeans, and a second-hand army jacket like Polo's. Cotton scarves wound around my neck. And I have decided to let my hair grow. It's either long or short in this environment, and the boys who wear it long, wear it *very* long.

I mailed that letter to my father the minute we arrived. The one that said I was having a holiday in a Swiss mountain resort and had met some charming people. I am tempted to phone him and say that I'm coming home. There is absolutely nothing to prevent me from going over to the Swissair office and buying my ticket.

Nothing but . . . Polo.

Ever since the night we kissed, I have thought of nothing else but making love to her, but it's strictly business with her now—our business being to shake off Gessner, Kubli, and the twins. I am sure that we have accomplished this, so why does she stick around?

The first night we arrived here, over dinner in the Neiderdorf, I told her some more about my life—about being odd man out wherever I went, and having no friends—and she understood. I told her how I had been named after the poet Archibald MacLeish, and how my father is such an eccentric, and what a drab milieu I live in. (She has never set foot in Queens, even though her dad has an apartment in the city. Park Avenue and 61st.) I told her about the cats, and about my school, and about you, Dr. Gutman. She could easily have been contemptuous of my story, but she wasn't. She listened and nodded. Once, she even touched my hand.

"We're both oddballs," she said. "That's why we like each other."

"Right. But you know—until recently, I didn't think you liked me at all."

"I identify with you," she said. "More than you know."

Back to Polo's friends. A boy named Nico, a boy named Hans, and two girls called Ulla and Lorrie. An older guy named Marcello who is gay. They are all different nationalities and seem to have come to Zurich to do away with themselves. I mean, they are high most of the time, and never get enough to eat, and don't always make sense. Polo says that they are all dropouts, of one kind or another, and have left their families far behind.

Nico and Hans each wear one earring in their left ear. Ulla wears a pants suit of dirty black leather. Her hair is punk and has a purple streak down the middle. Lorrie is English and very upper-class. Her accent is so beautiful that I can barely understand her. We have eaten a few meals with this group, and we have gone with them to the pinball parlors on the Limmatquai—where people buy drugs, cruise, or simply nod off.

The whole thing makes Queens look tame.

I've been longing to drop in at the Hotel Opera, to say hello to Marie, at the desk, but Polo says this is verboten. She says we must be cautious.

My latest thought is that "the goods" are spy secrets. Or perhaps a cipher machine that breaks codes. I read a James Bond novel once that concerned this kind of machine—and men were willing to die for it.

Does Polo care for me, Dr. Gutman? Most of the

132

time, I think not. But there are moments when I catch her looking at me in a strange way—as though she felt some tenderness. She is such a mystery! Tough one moment, gentle the next. . . . I am intimidated by the fact that she is experienced. How could I ever sleep with her, being a virgin? I would probably ruin the whole thing.

March 20 It is late afternoon and I am sitting on a bench in the Hauptbahnhof, the main railway station. Polo is bathing in the ladies' room (they have public showers here) and I am munching on a bar of chocolate and writing in this journal.

We took a streetcar up to the zoo today, on the Zurichberg, and the whole thing made me very sad. The place has decent accommodations for small animals—but the big ones are crowded and depressed. Panthers and leopards lie around on shelves in little cages. Lions just sit there looking at you. This zoo is the only attraction in Zurich that is not well done (I kept thinking of the Bronx Zoo), but the reason it depressed me so much is that it

133

made me think of the cats back home. Hans Christian and Lewie Carroll. L. Frank Baum.

Polo is having dinner tonight with the English girl, Lorrie, who is in some kind of trouble and wants to talk to Polo privately. I will eat at the Odeon and wander around the city.

March 21 THEY ARE HERE. Gessner, Kubli, and the two characters that Polo calls the twins. They attacked me last night—the twins, I mean—in a narrow lane near St. Peter's Square. If an American woman hadn't intervened, they would have kidnapped me.

It was around nine at night, Polo was off somewhere with Lorrie, and I was heading up towards St. Peter's Square, where the street musicians have been playing. The rain had stopped, and the city looked magical. An inky sky, and the lamps in front of buildings glowing softly. Group singing coming from one of the guild halls. The huge spire of St. Peter's rising above me, and its bell clanging the hour.

And then someone grabbed me.

I turned and saw that it was one of the twins. The male one. He had pulled my arms behind my back and was twisting them. His counterpart, the female, was standing a few feet away.

"The game is over," said the man, in some strange accent. "Either you produce the goods or you are a dead man."

"You're hurting me!" I said.

"The goods!" he growled in my ear.

"I don't have your goddam goods! I never did! I'm not Brian Chesterfield."

"We know that."

"I'm not Rick Olsen, either! My name is Archie."

"Tell that to Gessner. He is waiting for you at the airport."

Dr. Gutman—all of a sudden I went crazy. Because I had finally had enough. There was *no way* these maniacs were going to kidnap me. I had had it!

I twisted away from the man, turned, and punched him in the face. He looked astonished, and punched me back. Then I socked him in the stomach, hard, and he gasped. He grabbed me around the neck in a choke hold—and that was when the Americans appeared.

135

A man and a woman in expensive clothes. Going back to their hotel after dinner, perhaps. Walking innocently up the lane. They almost bumped into us.

"What are you doing to that boy?" said the woman. "Stop at once! You're hurting him!"

"Martha, please!" said her husband.

"No," she said, "he's hurting that young boy. You! Stop it now!"

She grabbed my attacker's coat and pulled on it.

"Martha, *please*," said her husband. "This is none of our business."

"But he's hurting him, John! You! If you don't stop, I will call the police."

Which is just what she did. She threw back her head and screamed, "Police! Help! We need help here!" and in about two seconds the twins had disappeared. "Are you all right, dear?" said the woman, patting me nervously. "Was he trying to rob you?"

To make a long story short, I told the Americans that I was fine, thanked them for their help, and went quickly up to the Square, where I sat down on the steps of the church and listened to the street musicians. I was shaking, but not because I was hurt. I was shaking because—for the first time in my life—I had fought back. From kindergarten onward people had been trying to bully me, and harass me, and beat me up—and I had never once raised a hand in my own defense. This time, I had.

Later that night, Polo and I sat on a bench on the Utoquai. She seemed very worried and was holding my hand. "You can't go to the police, Geraldo. You entered this country illegally. They'll put you in jail."

"I *have* to go to the police," I said to her. "There's no other alternative."

"Yes, there is. You could get a ticket and fly home."

"They'll follow me wherever I go. You said it yourself."

"Do you know that you have a black eye?"

"No."

"It's a real shiner. . . . Listen—do you think those goods they keep talking about are drugs? There's a big drug traffic in Zurich."

"I don't know. I just know that I need help."

"What about that woman you mentioned to me in Davos? Melina."

"I haven't been able to reach her."

137

"She lives in Zurich?"

"Yes. But she doesn't answer the phone."

Polo glanced at me. "Is she really your lover? You sort of intimated that she was."

"I . . . was lying to you."

"I see," she said quietly. "Look, Oscar, would you like to hop into Italy for a while? I'd go with you."

Suddenly I felt very tired and very old. "I don't want to run anymore, Polo. I can't."

"Poor kid. I feel for you."

I almost took her in my arms then, Dr. Gutman, but something held me back. The fear of rejection. The fear that I would make a fool of myself.

"It's funny," I said to her. "It's harder for me when you're gentle than when you're tough."

She smiled. "So you want me to be tough?"

"No. Of course not."

She kissed me then, and it was a kiss that went on for a long time.

"I know I give you mixed signals, kid. I'm sorry."

"It's OK," I muttered. My face was buried in her neck.

"I don't mean to do that. I mean, I *hate* girls who tease. I'm just confused, that's all. Too much too soon, and all that kind of thing."

138

I was stroking her hair, Dr. Gutman, and for reasons I cannot explain to you, I was close to tears. "You don't have to apologize. Really."

"But I hate teasing. And I really like you. More than you know. I'm just not ready to . . ."

"It's OK. I'm not ready, either."

"I wish I could come back to America with you. And go to your crummy high school, and take exams, and date, and just be a normal person. I'm so tired of being me."

I kissed her hair. "Which is why you pretend to be a hippie."

"Street person," she said absently. "The word hippie went out long ago."

I gave her a hug. "Let's go to the Limmatquai and have a pizza. And if the thugs show up, we'll buy them a pizza too."

Polo looked at me. "Oliver," she said, "I applaud your guts."

March 22 I am writing this at the Odeon, over a glass of wine. Polo is hanging out somewhere with Ulla and Lorrie, and they will meet me here at ten

P.M. I am very shook up because I saw Mrs. Mendel-sohn today. She was not at all what I remembered, and we had a very disappointing conversation. The weird thing is that we bumped into each other at the railway station. Or rather, *I* bumped into her. She did not recognize me.

OK, so I was dressed as a street person. But was that any reason for her to have amnesia? She couldn't even *place me*, Dr. Gutman. I have been having sexual fantasies about this woman for an entire month, and she wasn't sure who I was.

As usual, she looked glamorous—that fur coat, those high leather boots, those dark glasses—but she also looked old. At least forty. And it was clear, when I grabbed her arm, that she thought I was trying to panhandle. She said something in German and pushed past me. "Mrs. Mendelsohn!" I said. "It's me! Brian Chesterfield. We met on the plane."

She looked at me blankly, and then she put down the suitcase she was carrying. "Oh!" she said, clasping her hands to her bosom. "I do not recognize you. Forgive me."

I was so glad to see her that I almost gave her a bear hug. It was like being lost in the desert and

140

suddenly seeing your best friend, and an oasis, and a couple of healthy camels—all waiting in the distance.

Mrs. Mendelsohn was staring at me, so I said, "I'm in disguise. That's why you didn't recognize me."

"Disguise?"

"I got your postcard, at the Hotel Opera, and I've been phoning you ever since. I'm so glad to see you!"

I could tell that she was caught between two impulses—the need to go wherever she was going (she had obviously just come off a train) and the need to be polite. "I've been phoning you," I said again.

"You were going skiing," she said. "It was your first trip abroad."

"Right, right. And I got your postcard, for which I was really very grateful. But ever since then I've been in a bit of trouble."

Her eyes narrowed for a moment. "There is a restaurant of fast food over there. Come. We will have a coffee together."

A few minutes later we were sitting in a self-service restaurant, over cups of coffee. "I return from Lugano several days ago," she explained. "Then, up to Klosters, and now back to Zurich. I am on trains every minute."

"Is your cousin OK?" I asked. I was so happy to see her, Dr. Gutman. So relieved.

"Yes, yes, he is fine now. But I do not understand this costume you are wearing."

"I'm living like a street person at the moment. That's all."

Mrs. Mendelsohn stared at me. "How incredible. Don't you know that all of Zurich is being ruined by them? The graffiti, the drugs, the protest marches . . . all very bad."

"I know. But it's been necessary. You see—four gangsters are after me. They almost kidnapped me the other night."

Mrs. Mendelsohn raised her eyebrows. "Indeed?"

"Right. Four of them. Because what I never told you is that I'm here on someone else's passport. His name is Brian Chesterfield, but mine's Archie Smith. I live in Queens. I came here quite by accident, on Brian's passport, and then I got into trouble with a man named Gessner. He gave me a present of some boots, and all hell broke loose."

"Indeed," Mrs. Mendelsohn said again. There was an odd look on her face.

"I don't know what the boots are all about, Mrs. Mendelsohn, but ever since he gave them to me, I've been a hunted man. I mean, these thugs chased me all over Davos, and then back here to Zurich, and I don't even know why. It could be cocaine, it could be spy secrets, I mean, my God, it could even be *atomic* secrets, but there's no way of finding out. Polo and I don't know what it is. She's the daughter of a famous writer."

Mrs. Mendelsohn glanced at her watch. "My dear, I am on my way to an appointment. I know you will forgive me."

"What?"

"It was so very nice to renew this acquaintance. So pleasant."

She rose to her feet, so I did too. "You mean, you're leaving?"

"An appointment, my dear, and already I am late for it. Enjoy your stay in Zurich."

And then, Dr. Gutman, I realized that she thought I was nuts. She was heading out of the restaurant, so I ran after her. "Mrs. Mendelsohn . . ."

She turned and looked at me. And I must say, the

look on her face was not friendly. "I am going now, young man. Good luck to you."

So that was the end of Mrs. Mendelsohn and all my hopes for her assistance. When you come right down to it . . .

I have just noticed that one of the twins is in this restaurant. The woman. She is sitting over near the window, reading a newspaper and sipping a glass of red wine. She is dressed in a black suit and a raincoat, a black beret. And of course, she is here to spy on me. To hell with her! I will not be intimidated anymore! Let her sit there until she turns to stone. I will not be bullied.

And now Polo and the two girls are coming into the Odeon. They are laughing, and Polo's cheeks are flushed. How pretty she is! And how crazy of me not to have known it from the beginning. I am in love with her.

March 24 Dr. Gutman, I am on an airplane heading back to the States, and everything is over—my life in Zurich, my relationship with Polo. I am on a Swissair 747 jumbo jet, heading for Kennedy Airport in New York, and I am numb from the shock of it all. Who would have thought that it would end this way? Who would have thought that one stupid incident would end the only adventure of my life?

To go back to that night at the Odeon . . . the woman in the beret did not approach us. She simply watched. Polo and her friends joined me, we all had Cokes, and then the two girls took off and Polo and I were alone. I couldn't get over how pretty she looked, how glowing. And before we knew it, we were holding hands across the table. I was almost positive that she felt what I felt—that some new magic was happening between us—but I didn't say anything, afraid that I would spoil it.

"Clive," she said, "you have a funny look on your face. What's wrong?"

You, I wanted to reply. You are what's wrong— and also what's right. I am in love with you.

Instead, I said, "I have a funny look on my face because one of the twins is sitting across from us. The woman."

Polo frowned. "The bitch. Let her sit there forever. I don't care."

"Me neither."

"Those bums . . . why do they think they can

145

bully us? Listen! Let's treat her to a glass of wine. *That'll* shake her up.''

We paid the waiter to take the woman a glass of red wine, with our compliments, and when she glanced over at us in surprise, we smiled and nodded. After that, we rose to our feet and walked out of the restaurant. She did not follow.

All the next day I felt that something was going to happen between Polo and me. We kept holding hands on the street, and glancing at each other, and once she even kissed me—very quickly—on the mouth. There was a new tension between us, something very wonderful and very new. I just couldn't get over it.

Then it was eleven at night and we were bedding down in our sleeping bags on the Utoquai. The sky was deep black, sprinkled with stars, and in the distance we could see the lights of the city and all the church spires. At eleven, the bells began ringing.

I was just snuggling down in my sleeping bag, trying to get comfortable, when Polo said, ''Would you like me to come in with you, Archie?''

Well, I jumped—first, because I had not expected her to say this, and second, because she had used my name. Not Fritz or Clive or Geraldo, but Archie.

"Sure," I said, trying to sound casual. "Come on in."

She crawled in with me and giggled. "This is all very Hemingway."

"I beg your pardon?"

"Nothing. Just a joke. Is there room for both of us in here?"

"Sure. Make yourself comfortable."

"Do you want to make love with me, kid?"

I pulled her close to me. "Yes, Polo. Yes."

"I've never done it before," she said.

There was a long silence.

"I know," she said finally, "I told you all those lies. But I've never done it."

"Then why . . ."

"I don't *know*, Archie. I just have this bad habit of lying. To make people notice me, I guess."

"You mean, to make your father notice you."

"It's crowded in here, isn't it? Let me take off some clothes."

Which she did, Dr. Gutman. Everything but her underwear. She snuggled back in my arms, and I thought I was going to die. From the happiness of it.

"I've never done any of those things I told you,"

147

said Polo. "I mean, about the worst thing I do is shoplifting. Which is bad, I know, but I don't sleep around."

"Then who are Fritz and Maurice and Geraldo?"

"Guys who have tried to make out with me. But none of them cared about me, really. The first one who's cared is you."

I was kissing her now, very gently, but I did not feel gentle. I felt like I was going to explode.

"Are you a virgin?" she asked.

"Yes," I mumbled.

"And do you really want your first time to be with me?"

"Yes, yes."

"Do you have a condom?"

I felt myself blushing. "I bought some the other day."

She chuckled. "I thought you said you weren't ready for all this."

"I was lying."

"Me too, Archie."

We began to kiss, and very soon we were making love. And I did not ruin the whole thing, as I had feared. And I didn't hurt her, as I had also feared.

The whole thing just happened naturally and beautifully, and it was right.

We must have fallen asleep the minute our lovemaking was over—very deeply asleep—because neither of us saw the floodlights that had been turned on the park, or heard the rough voices of the police, talking loudly in Swiss German. We didn't hear or see anything, until the cops were right on us, shaking us awake. "Oh my God," said Polo. "It's a sweep."

"What?" I muttered. I was all tangled up with her, arms, legs, everything.

"It's a *police sweep*, Archie. They're going to take us in."

All along the Utoquai, the Swiss police were shaking people awake—kids, derelicts, lovers. And before Polo and I knew it, we were being pulled out of that sleeping bag, made to dress, and marched off to a police van. They had already frisked us for drugs, but of course we had none.

Which is what I kept telling them. But do you think anyone would listen to me, Dr. Gutman? They just kept shouting orders in their guttural Swiss German and loading people into vans. Some of the teenagers were laughing like it was the funniest thing in the world. Others were too stoned to do anything.

Since our van had no windows, I couldn't see where they were taking us. But we ended up at some big police station in the middle of Zurich. Then they were separating the boys from the girls. Polo hugged me quickly before she was taken into another room.

What I gathered from the kid standing next to me, who spoke some English, was that 1) it is illegal to sleep in the parks in Zurich 2) the cops conduct sweeps regularly 3) the penalties for drugs and loitering are very strict. "A friend of mine, he was carrying a little grass," said the Swiss boy, "just a few joints, you know. And they sent him to jail."

We were all in single file now, waiting to talk to the police officer at the desk, and panic was overtaking me. All my I.D. was in a locker at the railway station—but it was Brian's I.D., not mine. I had nothing on me to prove who I was.

When it became my turn at the desk, I tried to appear calm. "I'm American," I said to the officer in charge. "And I'm here on vacation. From New York."

"*Ja, ja,*" said the officer, looking bored. "Your passport, please?"

"It's in a locker at the Hauptbahnhof. But it isn't my passport, it's someone else's. I came here illegally a month ago. It wasn't planned or anything. It just happened."

The man was looking strangely at me. I couldn't imagine what he was thinking. "Your name, please?"

"Archie Smith. I'm from Queens, New York."

The policeman was studying me carefully. Then he said something in Swiss German to a man in plain clothes, a detective perhaps, and this man led me into a small office. He motioned for me to sit down, went over to a file cabinet and pulled out an 8×10 photo. It was a copy of a photo that sits in our living room. My dad took it of me last year.

"I don't understand," I said.

The man smiled. "Interpol has been in touch with this office for several weeks now, about a certain young man, from Queens, New York, who has been reported missing by his father. This is his photograph. Would you say that it is a likeness of you?"

"What's . . . Interpol?"

"The international police. Do you recognize the photo?"

"Yes. It's me."

"You make it easy for us by giving us your name. Very intelligent. But something I wish to explain here—this office has not been created to search for young Americans. That is not our job. Our job is to do with the city of Zurich, not with American runaways."

"I didn't run away," I said tiredly. "It just happened."

"Good, good. So tonight you sleep here, in jail, and tomorrow we put you on the plane to New York. We phone your parent and he will meet you. And all of this costs the Swiss taxpayer money. You understand? You run away from New York, and the Swiss people pay."

"But I didn't . . ."

The man took me by the arm and led me back to the main waiting room. Suddenly, I saw Polo at the far end of this room, standing with some other girls. I ran up to her. "Quick," I said, "write down all your phone numbers. They're sending me back to New York."

152

"Oh, God," she said. "They're sending *me* up to Davos. They already called my dad."

"We can't let it end this way! We'll . . ."

I never finished the sentence, because the detective walked over and took me by the arm. "No talking!" he said. "Talking is not allowed."

Polo had grabbed a piece of paper from someone's desk and was writing frantically. "These are the numbers, Archie. One in Davos, one in New York, one in Cannes."

She thrust the paper into my hand, and then the detective led me away. And that night, Dr. Gutman, I slept in jail.

(I have to pause here. My Swissair dinner is being served. It looks very good.)

OK. I've eaten now and can get back to my story. I slept in jail that night—badly—and was wakened early in the morning by a matron who gave me coffee and rolls. The detective, whose name was Shriker, turned up again and said that I was booked to leave for New York on the one o'clock plane from Kloten Airport. He said that two policemen would take me to the railway station, to get my possessions from the locker, and then they would drive me to the plane. "We have phoned your father," said Shriker, "and he did not speak—he wept. You should be ashamed for causing him such trouble."

I felt like I was in the middle of a bad dream. Forms to be filled out, and mug shots taken of me, and discussions between Shriker and the two cops he had chosen to take me to the airport. Then the cops and I were in a police car being driven by a third cop—and we wound up at the railway station.

Walking through that huge echoing station, with a cop on either side of me, I saw the whole adventure pass before my eyes. I saw myself arriving at the Hotel Opera with Mrs. Mendelsohn, afraid to go in. I saw myself standing at the top of the Parsenn, in the bright-blue cold. I saw myself sitting over a glass of wine at the Odeon, feeling *Zurichoise* and worldly. . . . One month, that's all it had been.

It had also been a lifetime.

Where was Polo? It was possible that she was right here, in this station, being put on a train to Davos by some lady policeman. I missed her so terribly! When would life ever reunite us?

The cops led me over to a wall of lockers, and I

searched around in my pocket for the key. My locker number was 506, and inside were all of my possessions. All of B.C.'s possessions, too.

The cops went to sit on a bench as I opened the locker and began to withdraw my things—the suitcase, the black purse, a small shopping bag full of souvenirs. And then, for a split second—out of the corner of my eye—I saw Gessner. He was walking through the station briskly, a package under his arm, and he was watching me. Yes, it was him. The brown leather coat, the beret.

For one crazy moment I wanted to run over and ask him to help me. But before I could blink my eyes, he was gone. He had vanished into thin air.

The two cops, whose names were Officers Wettstein and Keller, led me back to the police car—and we began our drive to the airport. It was eleven in the morning, and these sights from the car window would be my last of Zurich. "It shouldn't be ending this way," I said aloud, and Officer Wettstein stared at me. *"Was?"* he asked. "Nothing," I said. "Never mind."

The Old Town disappeared as the police car headed away from the railway station, into a neighborhood I had never seen before. The spires of St.

Peter's and the Fraumunster were disappearing too. As usual, church bells were clanging the hour, and it was raining again. Where was Polo now? Heading towards Landquart, preparing herself to face her father's fury.

Wettstein and Keller had been talking to each other in Swiss German. They seemed amused with their job of escorting me to the airport, and kept making little jokes. Wettstein lit a cigar and puffed away on it.

When we reached Kloten Airport, Keller explained that I would not be going through Passport Control, that they had arranged for me to go directly onto the plane. "Next time you run away, run away to *Geneva*," he said. The two men looked at each other and chuckled.

We were walking through the air terminal, the cops on either side of me, all three of us keeping step together. Walking steadily towards the escalator that would take us down one level to the plane—when I saw Gessner, Kubli, and the twins. They were standing by the escalator, and the look on their faces, when they saw the cops with me, was incredible. Their eyes opened wide as saucers. Gessner's mouth dropped open.

156

As we came closer to them, I could see the rage on Gessner's face. The other three just looked dumbfounded, but Gessner looked as though he could kill me. Yet there I was, being escorted to an airplane by two uniformed policemen. There was nothing he could do.

As the cops and I passed Gessner and his gang, to step onto the escalator, I nodded and said under my breath, *"Auf Wiedersehen*, Gessner." Then the cops and I were sailing downward. I looked back, and saw that Gessner's face was beet red.

Wettstein and Keller stayed on the plane with me until a few minutes before takeoff. I shook hands with both of them. "Remember," said Keller, "no more running away. Or, if you must, run away to Geneva."

So now I am over the Atlantic, Dr. Gutman, and instead of feeling relieved, I only feel that my life is in ruins. I have lost Polo, whom I love. I am returning home to a father who is in pieces and a school that will probably expel me. And the mystery of "the goods" is still unsolved. Will Gessner follow me to New York? And what about B.C.? I still have his traveler's checks and quite a bit of his money. I still have his little red address book.

<u>March 25</u> Midnight. It is *incredible* to be home. I can't get used to it—and after Switzerland, Queens looks awful. The streets littered with garbage, everything dingy and mean. I don't know. Maybe it's jet lag, but everything here looks dreadful to me. With the exception of my father, of course, and the cats. He was waiting for me at Kennedy Airport, and he hardly recognized me as I came towards him, carrying my suitcase and my shopping bag. "Archie?" he said. "Oh God, is it you?"

Well, of course I had changed a bit. I was wearing my street person's clothes, and my hair was longer. And I guess I looked haggard, too. He took me in his arms and wept.

I tried not to cry with him. Because I knew if I started crying, I would never stop. So I just patted him on the back. "It's OK," I said to him. "I'm fine, really."

He stepped back and looked at me. "My God, son, you look like a hippie."

"Street person," I said. "The word hippie went out long ago."

My father was not alone. Behind him, stood a man in an overcoat and a tweed cap. "This is Detective Burns," said my dad. "He's been helping me."

I shook hands with Detective Burns, who did not seem too friendly. "Tomorrow, when you're rested, we'll have a little talk," he said to me. "There are a few things we need to straighten out."

As soon as the detective left, my father took out his handkerchief and blew his nose. "The cats are in the car," he said.

"The *cats*? All of them?"

"No, no, just Lewie Carroll and L. Frank Baum. You know how they love to go for rides."

We walked out to a big parking lot, and there were Lewie and L. Frank in the back of our Chevrolet station wagon. I got in the car and stroked them. Lewie hissed. "He doesn't remember me," I said to my father.

"Of course he does, Archie. It's just that you look . . . different."

I sank back against the car seat. "I know."

But he looked different, too. Older than I had remembered, and very tired. There were pouches under his eyes.

We sat there for a while, Dad and I in the front

seat, and Lewie and L. Frank in the back. They were watching the cars go by. "It looks enormous here," I said. "I mean, Zurich is so small."

My father took my hand and held it. "Archie, I'm not going to ask you any questions now. Not till you've had a hot bath, and dinner, and a good night's sleep. Then we'll talk. OK?"

"OK," I replied. "Thank you."

He put the key in the ignition and started the car. "The Countess d'Aulnoy had kittens yesterday. I didn't even know she was pregnant."

"No kidding, Dad. How many?"

"Just two. She's an old girl, you know. This will probably be her last litter."

"You should have had her spayed years ago."

"I know. But her health was delicate then. I didn't want to."

He was pulling out of the parking lot, weaving in and out of traffic. "It looks so strange here," I said. "I just can't get over it."

So now I am sitting here in my room, which looks shabbier than ever, surrounded by all the old familiar things—the books and magazines and travel posters and piles of sneakers—and the only thing I am certain of is that nothing has been resolved. On

160

my desk is a book I was reading just before I left, a book on travel, and I see that I have marked a passage that says, "Many a world traveler departs in the hope of defining an unknown self—or abandoning a tiresome one—of being quite literally carried away. New aspects of a man can be released in the presence of the unfamiliar, the new and exciting, the strange."

Has that happened to me, Dr. Gutman? I'm not sure. But when I arrived in Zurich, I felt like a stranger in a strange land. And now I feel the same way in Queens. Also, I am no longer a virgin.

I have called Polo twice, at her number in Davos: No answer.

Perhaps the truth is that I am split in half now, a part of me glad to be back with my father (if not back in Queens) and the other part of me still in Zurich, on the Utoquai. Fog is drifting over the lake, and the light has a greenish glow, and the bells are ringing. Swans sail by in the gloom. . . .

This morning, over breakfast, my father asked me to tell him what happened—the whole story—but I couldn't. I just told him about B.C. falling to the floor in the Skyview Restaurant, and about how I took his passport and got on the plane. It was a

161

whim, I said, a sudden impulse. I can't explain it.

I said that I had been living with the street people in Zurich, that I had spent a few days in Davos, and that I had met a girl I liked. He knew I wasn't telling the whole truth, but I could tell he didn't want to push me. Then he threw me one from left field.

"I don't want to upset you, Archie, but you may be up on Federal charges. Over the passport."

I choked on the cereal I was eating. *"What?"*

"It's a Federal offense to use another man's passport. I've hired a lawyer to help us, and he may be able to get you off because of your age. But we'll have to see Detective Burns today."

"God!" I said. "I didn't know any of that."

"I've also made some appointments for you with Dr. Gutman. I think you need to see him very much."

"How are we going to afford all this?"

"Don't worry, son. We'll manage."

I glanced at him. "You went to so much trouble to find me."

"Trouble! I would have gone to the ends of the earth. I had already bought a ticket to Zurich, you know."

"Really?"

"Yes, for the twenty-fourth—which is the very day the Zurich police phoned me. I'd gotten a leave of absence from the college."

"You make me feel awful," I said to him.

He pulled me to him in a rough kind of hug, and then we drew apart. But it was true. I did feel awful. I had hurt him very much.

Today we had a meeting with Detective Burns, at the local police station, and there was a man from the U.S. Immigration Office there too, Mr. Lake. I told them the same story I had told my father, because I simply cannot go into all the complexities of Gessner, Kubli, and the goods. But I'll tell you one thing, Dr. Gutman, this is the last time in my life that I ever lie. The next time I go abroad, I will send printed announcements to everyone.

I gave Mr. Lake B.C.'s passport, money, traveler's checks, and all the other stuff. I kept his address book, though, because I need to *find* this man and resolve our difficulties. I need to know what "the goods" are and why B.C. was going to Zurich in the first place. The letter of reservation from the Hotel Opera, that was in his purse when I first

163

opened it, is addressed to Brian Chesterfield, 50 West 12th Street, New York City. But he is not in the Manhattan phone book. An unlisted number. Why?

Detective Burns said my case is now pending.

<u>March 26</u> I am writing this just before dinner. My father is cooking something that smells like beef stew, and there is a snowstorm raging outside. Snow! At this time of year. On the other hand, Davos is probably thick with it.

I am in luck as far as school is concerned—spring break started today. My father phoned the principal and said I would be back in two weeks. But I'll have to be tutored.

Everyone knows that I "ran away." It will be hard to face them.

Dr. Gutman, the only thing to do with this notebook, when I've finished writing it, is to give it to you as a birthday present. Because in our first session today, I was tongue-tied. "Look," you said to me, "it isn't a crime to run away. Many kids do it. Tell me what happened."

164

"I didn't run away," I said. "Anyway, it's a long story."

You looked different to me when I walked into your office, Dr. Gutman. Not as young as I remembered. Or as sympathetic. To tell you the truth, you reminded me of Wettstein, the cop who escorted me to Kloten Airport. Jolly, but with a fascist tinge. "Archie," you said, "we have got to talk. Your father has been out of his mind."

"It's a long story," I said again. You glared at me.

We will be having appointments twice a week now, until I open up to you. But I have the feeling that I never will. There is just something in your personality that I cannot respond to. Also—you cut your hair very short while I was away. You really do remind me of Wettstein.

I have been phoning Polo constantly. Finally, one of the maids picked up the phone and said, in very poor English, that Polo and her father are in Barcelona. So what do I do now, Dr. Gutman, head for Spain? All I can hope is that she'll contact me. But something occurred to me yesterday—which is that she never said she loved me. All during the night we were making love, I told her that I loved her. But she never said it back.

165

After dinner It's amazing the way my dad has been doing the cooking since I've come home. And he hasn't even asked me to help with the dishes! He is no longer treating me like a hausfrau.

Just opened B.C.'s address book and read through all the names, addresses, and phone numbers. Three women's names are underlined in red ink, so I phoned each of them. The first two refused to talk to me at all, even though I said I was a "friend of Brian's," but the third agreed. Her name is Shirley Malone.

At first, she was very reluctant to talk. I mean, the minute I said I was a friend of Brian's, she became suspicious. But then I took a chance—a big one—and told her part of the story. How Brian had fallen to the floor of the restaurant and how I had gone to Zurich on his passport. "My God," she said, "are you really telling me the truth? How old are you?"

"Sixteen. I go to Woodrow Wilson High School."

"And you went to Zurich on his passport?"

"Yes. On a whim. Listen . . . is he dead or something? Do you know?"

There was a bitter laugh on the other end of the phone. "No, he isn't dead. He's in jail. And, for

166

your information, what happened was that he took a handful of peanuts the night he met you—a handful of peanuts along with his drink—and had an allergic reaction. He called me to come to the hospital the next day, when he came around, and he was *frantic* about the loss of his stuff. The money and the passport, etc. But now he's in jail, so it's all over. I mean, who would have thought that Brian was a crook?''

"Did he know he was allergic to peanuts?''

"What do you mean, did he *know*? Would he have eaten the peanuts if he knew?''

"Can we meet somewhere?'' I said to her. "I have to talk to you. It's important.''

Once again, that suspicious note came into her voice. "Are you sure you're not a cop?''

"How could I be a cop! I'm only sixteen. I just told you, I go to Woodrow Wilson High.''

"Well . . . OK. I live at 146 East 92nd Street, in Manhattan. If you want, you can come over tomorrow, 'cause I'm not working at the moment. I am, as they say in the business, at liberty.''

What business? I wanted to ask—but didn't. "Thank you,'' I said. "What time do you want me to come?''

"Make it around four. But if you turn out to be a cop, you don't step a foot in here. Not without a warrant."

March 27 I saw her, Dr. Gutman, and in a few short hours the whole mystery was solved. Fortunately, my father had a committee meeting at the college, so I took the subway into town and caught a cab up to 92nd Street. Shirley Malone was waiting, and opened the door of her apartment very cautiously. Then she saw it was me. A sixteen-year-old person wearing a duffel coat and Ulrich Gessner's fur boots. The city is covered with snow, so I had decided to wear them.

She was pretty, in a loud sort of way. In her twenties, tall, with red hair. Her apartment was a mess, however. Cigaret butts all over the place, and magazines scattered about. There was a nightgown hanging over a lampshade, and a pair of shoes on top of the TV.

"Well," she said, studying me, "you really are a kid. But you don't look sixteen. You could pass for older."

"I know."

"So come in and take a load off. I'm curious to know what you have to say."

She took my coat, put it on the couch, and offered me a chair. It had some underwear on it, which she quickly removed. "Sorry," she said, "this place is a mess. But I make rounds all day, so there's no time to clean up."

"Rounds?" I said politely.

Shirley Malone lit a cigaret and blew a long stream of smoke into the air. "Yeah, rounds. I'm an actress. But at the moment, I'm at liberty. Which translated means—unemployed. You want a drink or something? A joint?"

"No, no, I don't want anything. But I really need to talk to you about Brian."

She lounged back in her chair and blew out another stream of smoke. "I'll bet you do. How the hell did you manage to go abroad on his passport?"

"It's a long story."

"It's illegal to do that, you know."

"I know. But I didn't then. Is Brian OK now?"

"The bum! Up to his ears in trouble, and he never tells me. We meet in acting school, right? A few months ago. And we do some scenes together and

169

then he starts coming on to me. So we have a few rolls in the hay—nothing important. But he tells me that his father is a stockbroker and that he's independently wealthy. And all the while, he's doing robberies on the Upper East Side, and selling coke, and committing all kinds of felonies."

"He's an actor?" I said. "I *thought* he was an actor."

"Right, an actor. But Laurence Olivier, he is not. He's simply a very good-looking guy who wants to be in the movies—when all along, his real talent is for being a crook. But do I know that? No. All I know is that he's a handsome dude with whom I have had a little fun. Anyway—the minute Brian lands in the hospital, he phones me to hurry over. So I do, and he's there with his face all swollen up, and immediately he starts to tell me the truth. How he's done robberies, and dealt cocaine, and how he has just missed out on the biggest deal of his life. A deal that involves some hoods in Zurich. And he's almost *crying* because he had that allergic reaction and wound up in the hospital. Right? Almost in tears because he missed his plane."

I was sitting on the edge of my chair. "Go on."

"All the time he is telling me this, I am wishing

that he wouldn't. Because I know it is leading some-where. And where it is leading is that he wants me to phone some guy in Zurich named Gessner, and tell him that he missed the plane. 'It was a huge deal,' he says to me. 'I could have made twenty-five thousand bucks.' "

"Yes?" I said. My voice was only a whisper.

"Now mind you, I am sitting there by the hospital bed and Brian seems lucid enough. But he is close to *tears* because of this missed chance to go to Zu-rich and pick up some goods. His job is to pick them up, and a few days later bring them back to New York. And for this, he will be paid twenty-five thousand. But at that point, the cops arrive, and right there—in the hospital room—they arrest him. Not for the Zurich deal, but for all the others. How they found him, I don't know, but suddenly he's under arrest—and *I* am being taken down to the police station for questioning. Me, who's never been in trouble in her life! I have an ex-boyfriend who's a lawyer, so I give them a piece of my mind about false arrest and all that. Not that I was ar-rested. Anyway, they let me go. But Brian, the bum, is out of commission. He's waiting indictment right now. The judge wouldn't set bail."

"Did you ever phone Gessner?"

"Not on your life! Because as far as I am concerned, Brian is a thing of the past. I mean, I may smoke a few joints now and then, but I do not want to be involved with criminals. . . . OK. So I've told you what I know. Now *you* tell me."

Dr. Gutman, I told her everything, every single detail of my adventure. The only thing I left out was Polo, because I felt it wasn't relevant—and also, because I felt it was private.

I talked for a long time, and when I finished, Shirley Malone lit another cigaret. She had been chain-smoking for forty minutes.

"God," she said, "what a story. It's so crazy, I believe it."

"It's the truth. All of it happened."

"And the passport and traveler's checks?"

"I handed them in to the police. Along with Brian's other stuff."

"Poor Brian. I almost feel sorry for him. I mean, twenty-five thousand bucks could have bought a lot of acting classes. Still and all, he wasn't a very good actor. In the sack, very accomplished, however."

I was starting to get a headache. "Shirley," I said

carefully, "do you happen to know what the goods are?"

"Of course I know!" she said. "The goods are diamonds that some international ring of thieves are smuggling into this country. Millions of dollars worth of diamonds that come from Amsterdam to Zurich, and then on to New York, where they are sold illegally. And Brian is *telling* me all this, just when I wish he wouldn't. Because I don't want to know. Not when it's diamond smuggling. No way."

"Do . . . do you know where the diamonds are now?" I asked her. My heart was beating very loud, Dr. Gutman, like a hammer.

"Stand up," Shirley Malone said to me. I did so. She looked at me carefully, from my feet to the top of my head. "If I'm correct," she said, "the diamonds are in your boots."

"WHAT?"

"For God's sake, lower your voice! You want the whole world to hear you? Stay calm."

"What do you mean, my boots? What do you mean? Are you crazy? There's nothing in my boots."

"Oh, yes there is, kiddo. Brian explained the whole thing to me. Take them off. I'll show you."

I unzipped my black sealskin boots and handed them to her. First, the right one. Then, the left. Frowning a little, she pulled on the crepe sole of one boot—and it came off in her hand. The sole of the boot was hollow, and inside it were a number of packages. Small, square packages, wrapped in tissue paper.

"Wow," she said. "He was really telling the truth, wasn't he? I mean, here they are."

She pulled the sole away from the other boot, revealing more little packages wrapped in white tissue paper. "So—shall we have a look?"

"I think I'm going to faint," I said. "Do you have some water or something?"

Shirley Malone hurried into her tiny kitchen and brought me out a glass of water. "Stay calm," she said, "stay calm." But she wasn't too calm herself, Dr. Gutman. She looked terribly pale.

After I had drunk the water, Shirley and I opened one of the packages. Under the tissue paper was a small plastic pouch—and in the pouch were ten diamonds nestled into wads of cotton. We held them under the lamp and they glistened. "How many diamonds do you think we have here?" I asked weakly.

"I don't know. Seventy or eighty. And they're all *cut*. I know enough about jewelry to know that these stones are cut."

We spread the diamonds out on Shirley's coffee table. There were a hundred of them. "God," said Shirley, "this is just what I don't need. A few million bucks worth of illegal diamonds."

"Why do you suppose Brian confided in you? In the hospital, I mean. You could have turned him in."

Shirley Malone thought this one over for a while. "The only thing that comes to mind is that he was desperate. And, hell, I'm a pretty loyal person when I like a guy. I guess he thought I wouldn't tell."

"I better go home," I said. "To Queens. I've had it."

"And leave me here with the loot? Oh, no you don't, kiddo! We're in this together."

"But I don't *want* the diamonds. Really."

"Well, I don't want them either, honeybunch. So we will just sit here until we decide what to do."

For the next twenty minutes, Shirley Malone and I sat there, staring at the diamonds that were spread out on her coffee table. "Look," I said, "couldn't we just mail them back to Herr Gessner? In Zurich?"

"Nope," she said, "too dangerous. Much too dangerous."

"Well then, why don't we put them in with your garbage and throw them out?"

"No good. Diamonds are the hardest things in the world. You can't just put them in the garbage. I mean, the garbage trucks crunch everything up in those machines they have, but diamonds wouldn't crunch."

"Could we bury them in Central Park?"

"Don't be stupid. With our luck, we'd get caught."

"I've got it! Let's drop them in the river."

Shirley gave me a cool look. "Which river?"

"The East River. We'll just stroll over and drop them in."

"Wonderful. In broad daylight, we go over to the promenade, lean over the railing, and drop them in. One by one, right? So everyone can see."

"Not that way! We put them in something—an old purse of yours, maybe—and throw it in."

"I've got a better idea," she said. "Wait here a minute." Upon which, she hurried into the bathroom.

When she came back, she was carrying an old

176

hot water bottle. It had once been red, but now it was a faded pink. "How's this?" she asked. "We put them in here, and then we *toss*. I mean, who will give a damn if they see us throwing a hot water bottle into the East River? They'll just think we're nuts, like the rest of New York. . . . Do you want a drink or something? I'm a wreck."

So we had a glass of scotch together, Dr. Gutman—and since I don't like scotch, I didn't drink much of mine. But Shirley Malone had two. "God," she said, sprawling on the couch, "what a scenario. Put it in a play and no one would believe it."

Around five thirty, we walked over to the promenade by the East River. It wasn't dark yet, and despite the snowy streets there were a lot of people around. Joggers, dog walkers, etc. Out on the river, bright little tugboats were passing. Shirley was carrying the hot water bottle in a shopping bag, with a towel over the top of it.

We went and stood by the railing. "It isn't exactly deserted here," I said. "I mean, people are jogging and everything."

"To hell with them," said Shirley. "We'll just stand here by the railing, and when the appropriate moment comes, we *toss*."

She giggled to herself, making me realize that she was a bit high.

"There are too many people here," I said.

Every time I thought it was going to be safe to throw the bottle into the river, some new person would appear—a fat lady walking a poodle, two girls jogging together, a businessman with a brief-case. "Now?" Shirley would ask, her hand slipping into the shopping bag. "No!" I would say. "Not yet! Wait till this woman passes."

The right moment just wouldn't appear, and after twenty minutes, Shirley became annoyed. "Look," she said, "it's cold out here. I've got to throw it in."

"Not yet! There's a man coming. No, two men. Not yet."

"So what do we do? Stand out here until our respective asses fall off? I'm *cold*."

"Wait," I said to her, "it'll be clear in a minute. Just wait. There's only one more person coming, a man walking a dachshund. After he passes us, we can toss."

The man with the dachshund approached, paused to let the dachshund pee, and walked past us. *"Now!"* I said to Shirley. "Toss it! Quick!"

With a look of fierce determination, Shirley reached into the shopping bag, grabbed the hot water bottle by its neck, and threw. She didn't drop it, she threw it—and I was amazed at how far it traveled. The only thing was . . . it didn't sink.

"Oh, my God," said Shirley. "It isn't sinking. It's floating."

"You're right! Why would it do that?"

"I don't know. We must have left a lot of air in it or something. It's all buoyed up."

"We can't just let it float away! We'll have to go after it."

She gave me a cold look. "Go after it?"

"We can't just let it float like that."

"What you are saying is that you want me to jump in and get it?"

"No, no, I didn't . . ."

"You are suggesting that I jump into the East River on a frigid day and retrieve that bottle? Or are *you* going to jump in? Better you than me."

The hot water bottle was far away from us now, being carried down the river by a strong current. It almost looked cheerful, bobbing along that way. "It's gone," I said.

179

We stood there until we could no longer see the bottle. It was traveling downtown, and was probably at 72nd Street by now.

"Whoever finds that bottle is going to get a hell of a shock," said Shirley.

"Maybe nobody will find it. Maybe it will just keep on going, out past the Statue of Liberty and towards the sea."

"Who knows?" she said, shrugging. "Come on, kid. Walk me home."

She seemed very depressed as I walked her home, Dr. Gutman. Thinking, no doubt, of the fortune we had just tossed away. Eventually, we stood outside her building gazing at each other.

"You know something?" I said to her. "It has just occurred to me that Gessner probably thought I was under arrest that day. At the airport. He probably thought the cops had found diamonds on me—and that I was being taken back to the States for prosecution."

"So?" said Shirley.

"So, if that's the case, he's no longer after me! I'm in the clear!"

"Good, good," she said. "So now I will say good-bye to you. And stay off airplanes."

180

"I beg your pardon?"

"Just stay off planes. European travel is not for you."

"Actually, it *is* for me. I'm even thinking of getting a passport."

She gave me a little smile. "Just be sure it's your own passport the next time. That's all I ask."

To my surprise, she leaned down and kissed me on the cheek. And then she was gone.

April 3 School starts tomorrow, Dr. Gutman, and I've gotten over my nervousness about going back. I will just go back and continue to run my life in its normal, solitary way. Because I'm still a loner, and probably always will be. One important thing has happened, however, which is that my case has been dropped. Detective Burns phoned my father yesterday to say that I would not be prosecuted over the passport—the reasons being my age, and the fact that it's a first offense.

I meant what I said to Shirley Malone. The next time I go, it will be on my own passport. You get them in the city, in Rockefeller Center.

I bought a book on Spain yesterday, and read all about Barcelona, where Polo is. How fantastic it sounds! An old seaport on the Mediterranean. Incomparable architecture by Gaudi. Roman walls still to be seen in the Old Town. "A dark, brooding romanticism," said the travel book. "A city of great mystery."

She hasn't written me once, Dr. Gutman—though I wrote two letters to Davos saying that I loved her.

After Detective Burns called, my father came into my room to tell me the news. Then he sat down on my bed and we talked for a while. He still doesn't understand why I ran away (so to speak) and I can't explain it to him. I mean, how can you tell a parent who loves you—who really loves you—that all you want in this world is to escape to some foreign place where adventure is waiting? How can you explain that home is all right, but that there's a whole world out there to be seen? Places like Barcelona and Venice and Dubrovnik. Places like Budapest. And even if I could find the right words, he still wouldn't understand—because home means so much to him. The security of it.

"I must have failed you in some way," he said. "Or you wouldn't have gone."

"It wasn't like that, Daddy. Really."

"I must have let you down."

"No. Honest. You didn't."

"I'm too involved with my own life—the college, the cats. But I'll try to be a better father to you in the future. I swear it."

But you're a wonderful father! I wanted to say. And it isn't *you* that makes me want to leave home. It's *me*.

You and I, Dr. Gutman, will be having two sessions a week right through the summer—and the thought is a depressing one. I mean, I don't think I will ever open up to you, so all we will be doing is wasting my father's money. I do intend to give you this notebook, however, when it's finished. And then you can diagnose me as being schizoid or something. Or having delusions of grandeur.

I wish that I liked you, Dr. Gutman, but I don't. Because when you come right down to it, I don't really approve of psychiatry. Its whole premise is that I am sick while you are well—and I don't believe that at all. In your own private way, you are probably just as peculiar as I am, only we don't talk about you. We talk about me.

I walked past my school this morning, just to see what the place would look like after a month—and it looked the same. Grim and shabby, its brick facade old and worn, its parking lot filled with refuse and cigaret butts. And then I passed the cement wall with the graffiti on it, the graffiti that says, "The best place to live is the ceiling." It was still there. No one had cleaned it off.

I stood looking at it for a while, and wondering who had put it there, and what he had been thinking at the time. It was possible that the person who had written it was someone like me, a loner, an oddball, an outsider. But whoever he is, Dr. Gutman, I wish I could talk to him. I wish that I could call him on the phone and invite him out for a cup of coffee or a beer. Because what I'd like to tell him is that the best place to live is definitely *not* the ceiling. Or even the walls or the floor.

The best place to live is the world.